STICKY FINGERS

VOLUME 6

JT LAWRENCE

FIRE FINCH

ALSO BY JT LAWRENCE

~

FICTION

FUTURISTIC KIDNAPPING THRILLER
WHEN TOMORROW CALLS
• *SERIES* •

The Stepford Florist: A Novelette

The Sigma Surrogate

1. Why You Were Taken
2. How We Found You
3. What Have We Done

When Tomorrow Calls Box Set: Books 1 - 3

~

URBAN FANTASY

BLOOD MAGIC SERIES

1. The HighFire Crown
2. The Dream Drinker
3. The Witch Hunter

4. The Ember Isles

5. The Chaos Jar

6. The New Dawn Throne

STANDALONE NOVELS

The Memory of Water

Grey Magic

EverDark

SHORT STORY COLLECTIONS

Sticky Fingers

Sticky Fingers 2

Sticky Fingers 3

Sticky Fingers 4

Sticky Fingers 5

Sticky Fingers 6

Sticky Fingers: 36 Deliciously Twisted Short Stories: The Complete Box Set Collection (Books 1 - 3)

Sticky Fingers: Boxed Set Collection 2 (Books 4 - 6)

~

NON-FICTION

The Underachieving Ovary

ABOUT THE AUTHOR

JT Lawrence is a USA Today bestselling author and playwright. She lives in Parkview, Johannesburg, in a house with a red front door.

www.jt-lawrence.com
janita@pulpbooks.co.za

facebook.com/JanitaTLawrence

twitter.com/pulpbooks

instagram.com/authorjtlawrence

amazon.com/author/jtlawrence

bookbub.com/profile/jt-lawrence

DEDICATION

This book is dedicated, with love and thanks,

to my Patreon supporters:

~

Joni Mielke

Elize van Heerden

Nigel Perels

Claire Wickham

Sian Kitsune Steen

Megan Guzman

~

Thank you also to my dedicated proofreaders,

Keith & Gill Thiele, and to all my loyal readers.

I wouldn't be able to do this without you!

STICKY FINGERS

VOLUME 6

1

EVERLAND

"We must check the sugar bowls for poison."

Derek gazed at the narrow winding road, and I could tell he hadn't registered what I'd said. He'd heard my voice, but his thoughts were elsewhere.

"Just kidding," I said.

"Huh?"

"I was joking. I said we should check the sugar bowls for poison. The Shirley Jackson novel, about the castle, you remember?" As the words left my mouth, the castle—*our castle*—came into view.

Strictly speaking, *Everland* was a manor. Still, it had all the beautiful features of gothic architecture with its grey stone and turrets, all kept safe under the watchful eyes of the resident gargoyles. Derek laughed at me when I called it a castle.

"We've bought a castle in the countryside," I announced to our friends over dinner, and Derek had guffawed.

"It's a manor," he had said, topping up our wine glasses.

3

I showed the pics of the building I had on my phone.

"Looks like a castle," they all said, especially with the seemingly ever-present fog that shrouded the tops of the turrets. It had thrilled our son Cameron; he couldn't believe his luck. Five-year-olds are like that with castles.

"You'll miss your friends in the city," I told him. "You'll be homesick. There's no McDonald's in the country."

This did not deter him. Who needs a Happy Meal when you've got secret rooms and attics to explore?

It was a sudden move, and I felt the whiplash. One week, Derek and I were young professionals in the city, the next, we had sold our business and our home.

"It'll be good to get away from everything," said Derek. I agreed. There was a lot of 'everything' we needed to get away from. The city was crowded with criminals and beggars and useless infrastructure. A hijacker shot our neighbour in his driveway. A colleague and his whole family had been held at gunpoint while a gang of five thugs invaded their house and ransacked it. It wasn't just the crime. There were other things, too; more personal things. Darkness. We loved the city, but we had to think about our Cameron. He was at such a beautiful, tender age.

While on a weekend break from the city we lost our phone signal and, without a map, got hopelessly lost. But the misty path had led us to the manor house; a FOR SALE sign staked on its front lawn. We were not usually impulsive, but Derek and I felt strangely drawn to the house.

"It'll be good for us," Derek said. "Healthy."

We traded a small neat backyard for sprawling green land populated by squirrels and chickens. In the city we had high walls and electric fences; the new property was hemmed in by fruit trees of every kind. There was no WiFi, no processed food, no touchstones to trip us up every time we saw something that reminded us of what we had lost. We could leave the difficult memories behind.

"I like this one," Cameron said, choosing the smallest, darkest room on the ground floor.

"Are you sure?" I asked. "The one near the staircase is much bigger." Our main bedroom was upstairs, and I wanted him a little closer by. "I like this one," he said again and began unpacking his things.

"Perhaps Cam can sleep in our room," I said to my husband. "Just till he settles in. I don't want him walking up those steps at night. He could fall."

"We'll leave some lights on," Derek said. He was better at hiding his tendency to be overprotective than I was. "Maybe the nightmares will stop, now that we're away from the city."

In the city, I worried about bullets and knives and car accidents. After we bought *Everland,* I worried about Cameron falling down the staircase in the middle of the night, and I worried about the expansive lawns and meadows that surrounded the castle. Where Cam saw giant trees, perfect for climbing, I saw him falling and breaking his collarbone. He saw rocks to clamber over; I saw a head contusion waiting to happen. He loved matches, candles, and the roaring fires in the stone hearth. I made sure all the matches and lighters were on shelves out of his reach.

"Promise me you'll never go near the river on your own," I said to him, holding his arms a little too firmly.

"It's hardly a river," said Derek. "It's a stream." Castle, manor. River, stream. I didn't care. I just didn't want my boy slipping on wet stones and being swept away. He couldn't swim.

"We've spoken about this," Derek said, gently. "One reason we moved here is so we wouldn't mollycoddle Cameron. He needs some space."

"He's five years old," I said. *Which five-year-old needs space?*

Derek fixed me with a firm look. "Let him be."

I didn't want Cameron to be so far away from us at night, in that small dark room, so we compromised; I set up the old baby video monitor so I could watch and hear him sleep.

"I'm not being paranoid," I said to Derek. "Just careful."

"It's okay," he said, hugging me. "It's okay."

The monitor added to my anxiety. Static would sweep over the screen; a wash of crackle and snow. I would jump up and search the monitor for Cameron's motionless form beneath his comforter.

"You should turn the volume down," said Derek. "You'll sleep better."

"I'm sleeping fine," I lied. If I turned the sound down, how would I know if Cameron needed me? But I took his point. When I looked in the gold-edged mirror, I saw my eyes bruised from lack of sleep.

"I'll get Mr Houndstooth to look at it," said Derek. "Perhaps there's a way we can get a better connection."

"Oh, we shouldn't bother him with that," I said. The groundskeeper gave me the creeps. He had brown teeth and a dirty coat and always stared at me suspiciously with his ratty eyes. The estate agent who had sold us *Everland* told us that the groundsman came with the house.

"We don't need a groundsman," Derek had said.

"Houndstooth comes with the house," the agent had reiterated and pulled his lips in a way that conveyed it was non negotiable. The price of the manor was less than half of what it was worth, and we wanted to secure the deal. We agreed in private that we could always come to an understanding at a later stage.

Mr Houndstooth looked at the baby monitor screen and banged the side of it.

"I've already done that," I said, in an attempt at humour. Houndstooth didn't smile. Instead, he checked the cables and then huffed his way down the grand stairway to Cameron's room. Once he'd checked the equipment there, he found me in the garden, cutting roses for the kitchen table while the hens pecked at the grass around my feet. He shoved his hands deep in his pockets and told me I'd need to buy a booster from town.

"While you're there," Houndstooth said, "buy some rat poison."

"Oh." I felt uncomfortable. "We wouldn't want that. We don't want to poison anything."

Not that I had a soft spot for rodents, I just knew the knock-on effects. I didn't want to accidentally kill any owls or cats. The groundskeeper hawked and spat on the ground. "Suit yourself."

He adjusted his hat and stalked off.

The town was a winding twenty-minute drive away, and our car's clearance was too low to make it a comfortable trip. We were planning on trading in our sedan for a Jeep, to better suit the terrain. Derek and I jokingly called the village a ghost town. There was one grocer, a hardware store, a barber, and not much else. It was dreary and bleak, but I didn't mind that too much. The worst thing about the village was the people. They looked strange, and they dressed in home-sewn clothes. They'd stare at me in a way that made my skin crawl as if they somehow wished me harm. Walking down the main road, we passed a blind man who looked at us as if he could see something, or someone. I squeezed Cameron's shoulder, and we hurried along. Cam and I bought the baby monitor booster from the claustrophobic hardware store with little trouble, although I felt uneasy with the way the shop assistant followed us around. Perhaps they were suspicious of city expats; thought of us as prior residents of a community rife with sin. The cashier in the grocery store ignored my greeting and glared at me as she rang up the items in my shopping basket, her bony hands working automatically to scan the barcodes. I busied myself with chatting to Cameron, ruffling his hair, reminding him to say "please" and "thank you". As I clipped my purse closed, the cashier grabbed my hand—a hawk clutching a mouse—and stared through me with electric eyes. Her cold skin startled me.

"You should never have bought that house," she said. Her teeth were sharp grey stones.

"Mom!" said Cameron, equally alarmed. He pulled on my arm. "Mom!"

I tried to snatch my hand away, but the claw held it fast. When I looked into the cashier's eyes, she finally let go, and we hurried out of the shop.

I set up the booster myself. It took over an hour, but at least I wouldn't have to see Mr Houndstooth again.

"Hello!" I shouted from our bedroom, eyeing the screen. "Wave at me!"

Cameron, who was in his room, below, looked into the camera and waved. "Hello, Mommy!"

The line was still a bit crackly, but we had a good picture, and sound, and I was happy with that. We ate dinner early that night—cottage pie with peas and carrots—and had a longer than usual story-time while a storm percolated outside our stone walls. I felt comforted with Cameron on my lap, a small body that had always been generous with cuddles and smiles.

At around midnight, I heard the whispering for the first time. I sat up.

"Can you hear that?" I asked Derek. He didn't answer, so I shook him awake and repeated my question. The wind was whipping tree branches against the manor walls, and thunder rolled and boomed in the lightning-scratched sky.

"Just a storm," he said, pulling me back down and slinging his arm over my torso in a sleepy embrace.

But it wasn't the storm. The thing I'd heard had come from inside, and it had sounded like a child whispering. I escaped Derek's slumber-heavy arm and went to look at the baby monitor, rubbing my eyes to dispel their drowsiness. The flagstone floor chilled my feet. I blinked at the jumpy picture; despite the fuzziness and flashing, I could see Cameron sleeping soundly. I felt so much love for him. He was such a beautiful boy, and we were so lucky to have him. I never took my son for granted. The screen fizzed again as the wind and branches blasted the castle. Satisfied that he was safe, I was about to turn back to my warm bed when I heard the whispering again. It was coming from the speaker of the baby monitor. A child's voice. I blinked again and stepped closer. Cameron's lips weren't moving. My nose was almost touching the screen when a new wave of static swept over it. I saw a small figure in the corner of the room, looking straight into the camera with shining eyes.

"Wave at me," she whispered.

Fright sent a power jet of ice water through my body. It felt as if my feet didn't touch the floor as I raced to Cameron's room and smashed the light switch on. I searched and searched, but there was no one in the corner. Cameron didn't wake up, despite the light shining in his face and the noise of my gasping. I clutched my chest—my heart vibrating beneath the bone—trying to catch my breath. When the shaking subsided, I scooped Cameron into my arms and carried him upstairs, placing him in the middle of our king-sized bed. I held him tight, watching him sleep as the storm gradually subsided, my mind fizzing like the picture on the snowy screen behind us.

"I know what I saw," I said to Derek the next morning as he made coffee.

"I don't doubt that you saw something."

"But?"

"But it could have been anything," he said. "You said, yourself, that the weather was interrupting the feed. Your mind was playing tricks on you."

"I saw a person," I said, and I felt my face pale as I remembered the fright of it. "A little girl."

"The human mind often interprets shapes as faces," said Derek. "And the whispering was the static caused by the electrical storm. I can see you got a proper scare. I'm sorry I didn't wake up."

The sun streamed into the kitchen, cheerful, as if it were an ordinary day. Frustrated and exhausted, I covered my eyes; scratchy from lack of sleep. Derek placed a mug of stovetop espresso with warmed milk on the table in front of me and then rested his hands on my hunched-up shoulders. The combination of sunbeams, the aroma of coffee beans, and his reassuring touch made my muscles relax. Of course it had been an illusion. The cashier at the grocer had shocked me, that was all. She had seeded a nightmare of repressed trauma. It all made sense in the daylight.

Derek let go and began rinsing the espresso maker in the vintage kitchen sink.

"Do you think we should tell him?" I asked. "Tell Cameron, I mean?"

Derek froze. The water streamed from the tap and swirled, untouched, down the drain.

"It's the right thing to do," I said. "Wouldn't you want to know?"

Derek stared at me for a while and shook his head. "No," he said and turned off the tap.

Later that day, I was walking around the manor grounds with Cameron. The property was huge and filled with organic snares: ditches; thorns; stinging nettles. We found the stream and watched the cold water gurgle by. I stopped to slap the ravenous mosquitoes attacking my ankles, and while I balanced precariously on one foot, I noticed a garden shed I'd never seen before, camouflaged in a carpet of moss and ivy. I called to Cam to be careful while he played at fishing, made my way to the hut, and wrenched the door open. The darkness inside glittered with golden motes. I had to step in to get my eyes to adjust to the dim light, but when I did, the rank odour of a dead animal assailed me. I gagged and turned away, wanting to escape, but the door slammed shut. I tried to open it, but it was stuck. I hammered my fist against the rattling metal.

"Cameron?" I shouted. "Cameron?" I worried about him near the water. "Cameron?!"

There was a squeaking sound inside the shed, and I knew without looking that it was a rat. More than one rat. I smashed at the door, but it wasn't moving. I pictured my son slipping on the shiny pebbles and falling into the stream, being swept away in its gentle pull. A rat tried to climb my leg, and I kicked it off. When my foot returned to the ground, there was a sickening squeal. I had accidentally crushed one of them. Another rat began to climb, and my skin erupted in welts I could not see. I screamed and ran my hands over my scalp, petrified that a creature would somehow get tangled in my hair. I pounded on the metal and tried to kick it.

"Cam!" I shouted, nerves like needles. Just as I felt my anxiety spiral out of control, ready to strangle me, the door scraped open. I launched out of the shed and straight into Mr Houndstooth. He grabbed me, and I flailed against his solid body.

"Let me go!" I shouted, and he did, causing me to fall backwards onto the weeds and rocks.

Breathless, I looked up at him, a monster in silhouette. I shielded my eyes from the sun so I could see his face. Some rats scampered out of the hut, and Houndstooth watched them with distaste.

I told you to buy rat poison, I imagined him thinking.

I got to my knees, and then my feet, clamouring over to the stream. Cameron was gone. I ran alongside the body of water, calling his name. Just as I suspected the worst, I saw him. He was walking into the water as if someone had hypnotised him. He was knee-deep, then waist-deep, then the water flowed over his shoulders.

"Stop!" I shouted, but he couldn't hear me. I saw his head go under the water. My mind crackled with panic. I sprinted towards him, slipping on the algae-painted stones and smashing down onto the rocks, cracking my elbow. The flare of pain didn't stop me from wrenching myself up again and splashing into the cold dark water into which my son had disappeared.

It was a small pocket of water, and his body was easy to find. He wasn't kicking or struggling at all. I grabbed his little body and hoisted him out, a howl escaping my throat. I carried him, scrabbling over the slippery stones and mud, almost falling again. Before I reached dry land, I felt his arms and legs coil around me, and he turned his cold face to me and buried it in the crook of my neck.

"Cameron! How dare you?" demanded Derek, who was beside himself with worry and fright at seeing his wife carrying his son's limp, soaked body up the lawn pathway. Cameron sat near the fire in the blanket I'd wrapped him in. We were all shaking.

"I'm sorry, Daddy," the boy said.

"You gave your mother a terrible fright," he said. "She's hurt her arm."

"Derek, please," I said. "It's nothing. Nothing compared to—"

"I'm sorry, Mommy," he said. His wide eyes filled with tears, and his face contorted in distress. I couldn't stand seeing his pain and rushed over to him, pulling him towards me. I began to weep, too. We had come so close to losing him.

"What on earth were you thinking?" asked Derek. His tone was less aggressive now, but it still resounded accusingly in the stone room. "You know you can't swim. You know you aren't allowed near that river."

"There was someone in the water," Cameron said.

"There was no one in the water," I said, as gently as I could.

"There was," he insisted. "When I looked down to see my reflection, it looked like me, but it wasn't. There was someone else there."

"No," I said. "It was just the light. The ripples."

"I knew you wouldn't believe me," he said. "But she was there."

My throat constricted. "*She?*"

"She's my friend. She comes to my room at night and tells me stories."

My stomach contracted sharply. "What kind of stories?"

"Stop your nonsense," said Derek, looking spooked. "Stop your nonsense this minute."

"But—" said Cameron.

Derek would hear no more. He left the room, leaving nothing but the silence of an un-slammed door.

That night I watched the baby monitor screen obsessively for the child in the corner; the little girl who almost drowned my son, but she did not appear. With the waves of pain emanating from my elbow, the shock and the sleep deprivation, I felt like I was going mad. When I looked in the mirror, a wild woman stared back. I forced Derek to go down to the stream where I had found the nightmarish shed strangled with weeds. It wasn't there.

"Fire him," I said to Derek.

"Who? Houndstooth?"

"He could have been the one who locked me in."

Derek took a deep breath. "You want me to fire the groundskeeper for perhaps locking you in an imaginary shed?"

My insides lit up with anger. "You don't believe me?"

He ran his fingers through his hair and looked around at the wild vegetation as if to prove his point.

"You think it was some kind of ... *episode?*"

"I think this move has been harder on you than you realise. You're not yourself."

I stood there, in the wild grass and weeds, wondering if I'd ever been myself. I wondered if I knew who I was at all.

The next afternoon I heard Cam crying before I saw him. I picked up my pace and found him in the workshop where Houndstooth kept his tools.

"What's wrong?" I asked him. "What's happened?"

"Houndstooth," sobbed Cameron. "He's a mean man."

"What?" I demanded. "Why? What did he do?"

Cameron just shook his head and sobbed. I stripped him right there, in the claustrophobic room that smelt like pesticides and petrol, and checked his body for any kind of bruising or damage. I found nothing out of the ordinary, except a box of matches in his pocket. I dressed him again, then I inspected the grimy workspace and saw a white powder sprinkled there. I knew, without a doubt, it was rat poison.

"You're fired," I said to Houndstooth on the static telephone line. At first, he was quiet, so I had to repeat myself.

"You're making a mistake," he said, his voice trembling with what I guessed was anger.

"I don't think I am. Collect your things, leave your keys, and then I never want to see you again."

There was an eerie silence.

"You'll be sorry," he said.

A few days later, Cameron told me he saw the groundskeeper lurking on the property. "What was he doing?" I asked.

"Nothing. Just standing and—"

"Standing and what?"

"Watching me."

A chill splashed my insides, and I had to sit down.

· · ·

Derek was furious that I had fired Houndstooth, so I tried to pick up some slack in the manor's maintenance work. Since we had sold our business, I found myself floundering. I realised work was essential to my mental health, so I threw myself into it. It also allayed my guilt at firing Houndstooth. I taught myself how to re-wire switches and fix dripping taps. I trenched flower beds and pruned the apple trees, and I paid Cameron to rake up dead leaves. The exercise was good for me, and I fell into bed exhausted at night, knowing I had accomplished something. I was sleeping well for the first time since we had moved to the country. After a particularly productive day mending and cleaning the chicken coop, I fell into a deep, dreamless sleep. At midnight, I woke up with a start. I felt a cold weight on my chest. I bolted up in bed, and the exhalation following my gasp was a white mist. I twisted my neck to look at the monitor and blinked. Gasping again, I flew out of bed to get a closer look, and the wave of cold air nettled my skin into gooseflesh. Cameron's bed was empty.

"Derek!" I shouted. "Derek! It's Cameron."

An eerie sense of *deja vu* hit me and trailed with it a cold, stagnant dread. I shook it off and hurtled downstairs, calling my son's name. Shivering with fright and cold, I switched his light on and checked the room, hoping I had imagined the empty bed on the screen. I had not. I called for him repeatedly, rushing from room to room and cursing myself for the unnecessary number of rooms we had. Derek crashed around the house behind me, opening cupboard doors and shouting for Cameron. I was freezing despite the heat of anxiety pricking my chest and scalp.

"He's not in the house," said Derek, his mouth slack with terror.

"Of course he's in the house!" I shouted. I had checked the locks twice before turning in, but when we got to the kitchen, we saw that back door swinging gently in the breeze.

"I locked this door," said Derek.

In my mind, I pictured Houndstooth's bunch of keys, a filthy leather tag as a keyring.

No, no, no, I panicked.

"Houndstooth," I said, my whole body shaking. "Houndstooth has taken him."

Derek tried to call the emergency service, but there was no signal. He ran up to our bedroom to try with my phone while I grabbed a flashlight and ran outside, calling for Cameron.

Had that awful man taken my son? Was he trying to exact revenge for my firing him? Fear bloomed like ice crystals inside me, cutting into my heart and lungs. I tried to bring my breathing under control, tried to think of the best plan to find my boy, but the static of the baby monitor screen had moved into my brain, and I found I couldn't think clearly past the blizzard.

I jogged haphazardly through the back garden, to the stream, sweeping the flashlight-beam as I went. I tripped over stones and tree roots but didn't fall.

"Cameron!" I kept shouting, not recognising the sound of my voice. I couldn't see him at the water's edge. I followed the trickling water; desperately searching. After what felt like hours, my feet were aching bricks, and my body was insisting on rest, but I ignored it. My mounting panic energised me. Finally, I heard what I thought was a child's murmur. There was a movement behind a bush.

"Cameron?" I yelled, my voice hoarse from calling. I rushed to the where I thought the sound had come from, but I couldn't see him; just trees standing like motionless people in the moonlight. Just black bushes and wild grass. The next step I took sent me tumbling into a pitch-black pocket as if the earth had swallowed me up. With a skull-shaking thud, I was at the bottom of a deep pit. I could tell from the newly chopped roots in the walls that it had been freshly dug, and it just happened to be the right size for me—that is, deep enough so I couldn't climb out. The bulb faded and flickered out, probably because of the fall. I shook it and slammed it on my palm, but it was dead. Everything disappeared into the dark, everything but my frantic breathing.

"Cameron?" I shouted. "Are you there? I need help!"

There was someone up there, then a scraping sound. A shovel forced its way into the earth, and the first load of soil rained down on me. I screamed, but the soil kept coming. Someone was going to bury me alive.

I don't remember what happened next. Derek thought I must have passed out from the panic. But I somehow escaped the hole because he found me wandering in the dark outside the house. He'd found Cameron inside, after all, curled up into a little ball, under his bed. You'd think he hadn't been outside at all if it weren't for the soil smears on his feet. Derek ran a bath for me; he washed the sand off my skin and out of my hair while I cried.

I couldn't make sense of what had happened. I went looking for the hole at sunrise, mist shrouding the castle grounds. The hole was gone, and Houndstooth's polished shovel was in the shed. I thought of his dirty coat and patronising sneer. The sound of his voice when he said *You'll be sorry.*

"He's trying to drive me crazy," I said to Derek. "First, the shed. Then the hole."

"Houndstooth?"

"Of course, Houndstooth! He's the only one, apart from us, who has keys to the house."

Derek frowned at me.

"Don't look at me like that! How else do you explain it?"

"I don't know," he said, shaking his head. "I don't know."

I made Cameron scrambled eggs and buttered toast soldiers for breakfast. Neither Derek nor I had an appetite, so we shared a mug of black coffee.

"Cameron," I said, speaking past the constriction in my throat. "What happened last night?"

"Nothing," he said, scooping the eggs up onto his fork.

"You went outside," I said.

He looked up at me, blinking, his face blank. "Outside?"

"When Dad found you, you were sleeping under your bed."

He shrugged. "I don't know."

"You don't remember going outside?"

"I remember my dream."

I tried to swallow the stone in my throat, but it was stuck. "What happened in your dream?"

"Victoria had something to show me."

There was a sudden searing heat on my stomach and in my lap. It took me a moment to realise I had spilt the coffee all over myself. I gasped and jumped up. "What did you just say?" I whispered.

Cameron's eyes grew wide, and he dropped his fork. "Sorry, Mom."

"What did you say?" I asked again, my scalded skin glowing.

Derek was motionless, pale, frowning at our son.

"Victoria?" I demanded. "Is that the little girl who visits you at night?"

Derek stared askance. He hadn't seen the girl on the baby monitor screen.

"Cameron?" I said. "Speak to us. What did you mean when you said—"

The air was vibrating with tension.

"Nothing," he said, and left the table, leaving Derek and me to stare at each other, horrified.

Exhausted and on edge, I spent the day vacuuming and tidying the attic. I filled it with books and toys, and a cupboard full of snacks. I hauled Cameron's mattress up there, and his favourite plush puppy. I installed the baby monitor camera and booster so I could watch him sleep.

"We can't keep our son locked in the attic," said Derek, scrubbing his scalp with the tips of his fingers.

"It's only till he's out of danger," I whispered.

"And when will that be?"

I lost my temper. I threw down the bucket I had been holding, shocking both of us.

"What do you want me to do?" I demanded through jaws wired shut with frustration. "Houndstooth is out there. He has keys to our house."

We didn't mention Victoria. We were both in shock.

Cameron played happily in the attic for a few days. He'd go digging in the old chests and boxes filled with the things we had yet to unpack. I'd take him out for a run around the garden, but I never let him out of my sight, and we no longer visited the river. One day when I took his lunch up to him, what I saw almost made me drop the tray. "Where did you get that?"

He looked up at me, holding the little yellow polka dot dress. A brown box lay open on the attic floor. The box I hadn't realised was up there.

"This is what she wears," he said. I slammed the tray down on the desk and grabbed the dress from his hands, locking the door on the way out. Derek took him his dinner.

Thoughts and memories rushed through my head like the babbling brook outside. I pushed the sad thoughts away. The castle was supposed to be a new start, away from the trauma of before, but my mind would not let the dark thoughts go.

"We need to tell him," I said to Derek. "And we need to get out of this house."

Derek sighed. "We can't afford a new house. And no one will buy this one."

"Speak to the agent."

"I have spoken to him. I spoke to him after the first incident. The baby monitor incident."

"So you believed me?"

"I don't know what I believe. All I know is that the hair on the back of my neck sticks up every time I walk into this place. We can't stay here, but we can't afford to move."

"We'll stay in a hotel."

It was desperation talking. I knew there was no money for a hotel. We weren't earning an income, and all of our savings were tied up in the house.

I felt like I was choking. "Cameron found her dress in the attic."

"What?"

"Victoria's dress. The yellow one."

I don't know why I said "the yellow one". It's not like we had kept any other clothes of hers. The polka dot dress broke our hearts because she had never grown into it. I had spotted it before I was pregnant and bought it without hesitating. It was the epitome of the happy future I had imagined for Derek and me; a ray of sunshine never realised. We had never told Cameron about his twin sister dying in her cot. We thought we could leave it all behind, but we were wrong.

"Do you smell something?" I asked. Was there the scent of smoke, or had I finally lost my tenuous grip on reality? Derek stopped and sniffed the air, then his expression crumpled in worry. I rushed to the front door, but it was locked, and the key was gone. The back door was also bolted.

"We're locked in," I said, my mouth dry.

We ran up the stairs and sprinted for the attic where we saw smoke unfurling from the bottom of the door like a grey silk sheet. I knew before I tried the doorknob that the door was locked. There was a searing pain and a hissing sound; my hand came away branded by the handle. I held my wrist and cried out in pain and terror.

"Cameron!" Derek shouted, and hammered on the door. His eyes were streaming.

"It wasn't me!" shouted Cameron, crying and coughing.

I remembered the box of matches in my son's pocket; the reason Houndstooth had reprimanded him, and then I understood a slew of things I had not yet been ready to see before that moment, caught in the crosshairs of love and terror. I saw it all now, and the fear almost flattened me.

Derek began kicking the door, but it wasn't budging.

"Axe," I gasped. "Get the axe. In the workshop."

Derek flew down the stairs.

"Cameron?" I shouted in a shaking voice. "Cam? We're going to get you out of there. Put something over your mouth so you don't breathe the smoke." There was no answer. "Cam?"

I felt my sinuses sting, but I was too shocked to shed any tears. I couldn't believe it was happening. He would have been safer in his stonewalled bedroom than in the timber-trussed attic. My eyes were swelling; I began to see stars. Derek was taking too long. I needed to fetch the axe, myself.

"I'll be back! I'm coming back! We'll get you out of there!"

I imagined his small body passed out on the floor, and the adrenaline pushed me down the stairs, coughing and spluttering.

It wasn't me, Cameron had said, and I knew he was telling the truth; a version of reality where impossible things happen, like a little girl ghost who leads her surviving twin brother into danger. Houndstooth had never been the dangerous one. It had been Victoria all along.

Derek lay unconscious at the foot of the stairs, a halo of liquid crimson around his leaking head. Later he would say he tripped over something he didn't see, and people wouldn't understand that, but I would, because I knew Victoria would do whatever it took to keep Cameron in that room until he died. She needed him to die; she wanted him to join her in *Everland.* That's why she took him to the deepest part of the river—hoping he would drown—and why she tried to get him to fall into the hole in the garden. I had saved him twice, but it had not been enough. Even if we got out of this godforsaken manor, she would forever be there, tempting him into peril.

As I stepped over Derek's body, a flash of guilt shot through me. I needed to stop and see to him, but I also needed to get the axe. When I reached the back door, I looked for something to barge it open with, but came up empty-handed. My panic stopped my brain from working, and I didn't know what to do next, except beat the door down with my bare hands. I pictured Cameron's body lying on that attic floor, soon to be devoured by Victoria's hungry flames. I used all the strength I could muster, and I ran against the door, smashing my shoulder into it again and again. When I heard my arm break, I switched my efforts to kick the door with all my might. My arm began to ache in a deep, dark way, but I kept up my assault on the door. I was weeping; hopeless. I was sure the attic was already a furnace by then, and I didn't know if Derek was still alive. Even though I felt the flood of despair, I couldn't give up. It was as if my whole life and everything in it came down to this one moment where I could turn our fortunes if I tried hard enough. I couldn't give up, no matter how broken my body felt. There was a small amount of power in the feeling.

It was the exact opposite of the feeling I had on the morning five years before when I had found Victoria lying in her cot, blue-skinned and breathless. Cameron had woken early and was sobbing in the cot next to hers as if he understood what had happened. My poor little Victoria; there was nothing I could do to save her. I was too late for anything but the overwhelming feeling of futility and heartbreak. The shock had blackened my insides for years, but my love for Cameron healed me. Finally, the screws holding the lock in place gave way, and the door flew open. I sprinted out into the night air, gasping for oxygen to fortify me. Suddenly there was a shadow the size of a bear. I recognised the smell of his dirty coat.

"Houndstooth!" I croaked. "Fire! Cameron's locked in the attic!"

We ran to the workshop together. I passed him the axe, and a mask to cover his nose and mouth. We hurried into the manor and up the stairs. I coughed as the thick smoke cascaded into my lungs. I wanted to shout for Cameron, but I couldn't catch a deep enough breath without choking. My eyes were almost swollen shut. Houndstooth let out a roar and began hacking at the door, razing it in seconds. The extra oxygen we had introduced into the attic made the flames leap towards the trusses. The curtains were already on fire. Cameron lay in the middle of the floor, exactly as I had pictured him. Houndstooth scooped his limp body off the floor. I was so grateful, sobs bubbled up in my throat. We made our way through the bitter smoke, down the stairs, where the groundskeeper passed Cameron to me while he lifted Derek and levered him up onto his shoulder. We walked over the splinters of the back door and out into the vast garden, black and beautiful and fresh under the moon. Houndstooth laid Derek down on the grass and listened for breath. I stared at him until he looked at me and nodded.

"Alive," he said.

I looked down at my son in my arms, skin powdered with soot, and felt his wrist for a pulse and wept in relief. I hugged him closer and nodded at Houndstooth. *Alive.*

Houndstooth's face melted in relief. It was then I understood that Houndstooth had known Cameron was in danger all along and had been watching him, hoping to keep him safe. It's why he had tried to take Cam's matches away from him. He knew what the house was capable of. It was a portal, a doorway, an alarm bell that unsettled spirits and brought them to the surface like dead fish in a stream. Houndstooth came with the house because he knew this; he was the guard. His eyes were haunted with the things he had seen.

We sat on the grass, watching the house burn.

"You removed that shed in the garden," I said. "The one I was locked in."

"Yes," said Houndstooth. "It wasn't safe."

"And you're the one who helped me out of the hole. You filled it so I could climb out."

"Yes."

"I thought you were burying me alive."

"I wasn't," he said.

"And that day that Cam said you were mean. It was because you stopped him playing with poison."

"And matches," Houndstooth nodded. "I tried to take them away. I know the dangers of this place. Easy thing to land up in the wrong hands."

"It's my daughter," I said, and his eyes flickered with emotion.

"I guessed," he said. "They have a strong connection. The boy and her."

"He doesn't know he had a sister."

The groundskeeper looked at me, and I saw the flames reflected in his eyes. "Yes, he does."

Despite the heat, my blood ran cold. "Victoria won't give up, will she?"

Houndstooth shook his head.

"She'll keep trying to get him to cross over to be with her."

"That's my understanding, yes," he said. "There's only one way to save him."

The realisation of what I had to do struck me like a lightning bolt; like the shock I'd felt when I'd found baby Victoria lifeless in her cot that strange dawn. It was blinding, and there was so much pain—as if it had sheared my body in two.

Derek began to cough.

"I need to go before he wakes up," I said, and Houndstooth's mouth turned down as he gave a slow nod. My throat burned with emotion. "You'll look after Cameron?"

"I will," said Houndstooth.

I uttered my thanks, hugged my unconscious son one last time and kissed his forehead, my heart bursting with love and grief, then laid him down next to his father, whose hand I squeezed in farewell. Tears streamed down my cheeks. The core of my body was glowing with a pain I had only ever felt once before, and I would never feel again. I gazed longingly at my family, and walked into the fire, to join Victoria in Everland. I'd keep her away from Cameron. My heart was aflame. I was burning up from the inside and didn't notice any pain from the fire that ensconced me. When I glanced back to get one last look at my family, all I saw were flames.

2

A HOMEMADE COFFIN

ROBIN SUSMAN CRADLES the calf in her arms. The animal's mother had rejected her; turned her away from feeding. Usually, nature has its own way of dealing with such things—a cruel reality that asserts itself often on a farm like this. Susman's neighbour, a third-generation cattle farmer, tells Susman she's too soft with the animals.

"Put it out of its misery," he'd say. "No point in keeping substandard stock." As if the weak calf was a faulty product you could dispose of, just sweep off the shelf and into the bin.

And yet here the creature is, in her lap, gulping down the milk from the bottle Susman had prepared; its survival instinct stronger than life's inherent cruelty. Damaged goods, Susman thinks. She can relate.

When the phone rings, Robin knows it is De Villiers. He's one of the few people who have her number. She also knows that someone has died.

"Who is it?" she asks him. "Who died?"

"We're not sure if she's dead."

"Okay," she says. What she means is: *You'll see.*

"Perfect case for you," says the captain. He makes it sound as if she enjoys learning about missing women. As if she'll jump at the chance to drive into the savage city that took everything from her.

Robin turns and gazes out of the window. Red soil, cloudless sky. "It's calving season."

De Villiers hesitates. "Will you come?"

"There's a calf here that needs me."

"There's a missing woman here that needs you more."

What Susman doesn't say: *The calf is still alive. I can make a difference to the calf.*

Ex-detective Robin Susman arrives in Johannesburg feeling resentful and tired after the drive. She's getting older; the journey is getting harder. She rubs her knees. Since when did driving make her knees ache? She spends a moment feeling powerless against the relentless surge of time; a torpedo with miniature grapple hooks that pull at your skin, hair, muscles, bones, psyche. *What is the point?* she wonders, as she takes in the visage of the smoky grey city. *What is the point of anything?*

De Villiers meets her at a coffee shop and greets her with a nod. It means: I appreciate you coming. I would hug you if it didn't make you flinch. I wish you lived here in the city instead of on that *fokken* farm of yours in the middle of godforsaken wherever.

"How are you?" Robin asks when they sit down.

"You know," Devil says, eyes bloodshot. "Overworked, underpaid."

"Same as always, then," says Robin.

Devil nods. "Same as always."

He opens a file and spreads the photographs on the café table. "Felicia Heddon."

The missing woman smiles at Robin, but the smile does not reach her troubled green eyes.

"This time, it wasn't the husband," said De Villiers. "She's single."

She was single, thinks Susman. "Signs of a struggle?"

Devil shakes his head.

"Threats? Restraining orders?"

"No, nothing like that."

"So, Felicia Heddon just disappeared into thin air?"

It was true that missing people fascinated Susman. How a human body, seventy-or-so kilograms of flesh and blood could vanish, seemingly without a trace. Children snatched away from parents; women who are never seen again; men who go to work one day and never come back. But no matter how careful the abductor was, no matter how meticulous the killer was, there was always a trace left behind, some kind of arrow, some clue. Magnetised iron shavings pointing in the direction she needed to look. Whether they were fortunate enough to find the clue was another story altogether. Susman blinks at the captain. "Have we got anything at all?"

"Nothing," says Devil. "Nothing was missing from her house as far as we could tell, not even a toothbrush. And no apparent reason for her to leave. Stable job, no excessive debt. No obvious stresses. We've asked for her medical records."

He orders another round of coffees.

"Friends?" asks Susman.

"What?"

"Did she have friends?"

"None that we could find."

"Who reported her missing?"

"Her colleague, or her boss. Not sure. Someone at work."

That's sad, thinks Susman. No one to report you missing except the person who needs their email responded to. Almost as pitiful as a woman with achy knees who bought a sheep farm in the middle of the Free State to escape her demons. Of course, demons have a way of following you, even if you sell everything you own and start a new life somewhere else. Demons like the dark nights in the country, where the night is as thick as molasses. They have more power in the long quiet nights of nothingness.

"Susman? You okay?"

Robin snaps out of it. "I'm just thinking."

"What are you thinking?"

"No one would miss her. Maybe her killer knew that."

Robin feels a heaviness in her lungs; a boot stamping down on her chest. Her hand moves up to her throat. Darkness leaks into everything. She tries to push down the cold blackness so that she can breathe.

"She's underground."

"A basement?"

"I'm not sure."

"Maybe she was buried. Or suffocated."

De Villiers knows better than to ask Susman how she knows that. He's used to her unnerving hunches; relies on them.

"Who are we interviewing?" she asks.

Devil looks at the scuffed face of his watch. "Carlos Amada. The ex-husband."

Susman and De Villiers pull up to a security complex in Sunninghill Estate. It's modest, with paint streaked by rust and rainwater. The guard gets Amada on the phone, and the black gate rolls open. Felicia Heddon's ex-husband waits for them in the sun-baked parking lot. He's wearing a shiny tracksuit, and Robin gets the feeling that he has dressed down to appear unworried. Looking anxious might make the cops suspect him, so he's gone for athleisure, despite it being the middle of a workday.

"Day off?" Susman asks him. He peers at her, eyebrows meeting in the middle of his tanned forehead, trying to size her up; perhaps trying to determine if she's a threat.

"Working from home," he replies. He invites them in and offers them coffee, which comes out of an espresso pod machine. Susman feels grateful and judgemental at the same time. Good coffee is a rare and prized possession, but as the used tin pods tumble into the rattling canister, she knows they'll end up in a landfill and take centuries to melt back into the earth. Carlos Amada cares more for his own personal comforts than he does for others. Susman wouldn't be surprised if he ordered bottled water at restaurants instead of tap water.

The house is cluttered with children's things—backpacks with fluffy keyrings, inside-out jerseys, a tablet with a cracked screen. Bright orange grinning jack-o'-lantern buckets still cradling cheap sweets. Four bedrooms and an office. The decor is mismatched and dated. Amada has money, but not enough. He'd like a bigger house, for one, and more domestic help. He'd like to have more space and tablets without cracked screens.

They settle on the patio beneath a garden umbrella. The small lawn is a tangle of toys.

"When is the last time you saw Felicia?" asks De Villiers.

Carlos bites his top lip while he thinks. "I don't know."

"You don't know?"

"We don't see each other much." He taps his fingers on the table and then holds his chin. "Actually, to be honest, we actively avoid each other."

"She reverted to her maiden name," says Susman.

"Can't say I'm sorry about that."

Susman doesn't break eye contact. "So you'd describe your relationship as acrimonious?"

"In polite company, yes," Amada says and chuckles to De Villiers, who doesn't return his mirth. Amada wants male solidarity; an unspoken agreement that women are more trouble than they're worth. De Villiers' face is stone.

"Why was your relationship problematic?" asks Susman.

"Honestly?" he says and ruffles his hair. "Felicia's a total bitch. When I heard she was missing, the first thing I thought was good riddance."

Susman blinks at him. "You were happy to hear she may be in trouble?"

"Look, lady," Amada says. "If you knew her, you'd understand. Felicia's always in trouble, and it's all her own doing. Yes, I was happy. I thought she'd finally moved away. Better for us. Better for everyone. It's not the first time she's just left without telling anyone where she was going or when she'd get back. I don't know where she's gone, but I'm hoping she'll stay away."

"She's been missing for six days," says Devil.

Carlos Amada gulps his coffee. "It's different, now. Obviously, I'm a bit worried now."

Now that you're the prime suspect, thinks De Villiers.

"I remember now," Carlos puts his mug down. "I know when I last saw her because we had an argument. A big argument. In fact, I can tell you the date, because it was on Halloween."

"What was the fight about?"

"Ugh," Amada says, pulling a face. "It was just Felicia being Felicia. She showed up drunk, wanting to take the kids trick-or-treating. It happens sometimes. She gets these romantic ideas in her head that she's a good mother and then shows up out of the blue after sucking down a bottle of wine at lunch."

"So, you told her she couldn't take the kids."

"Let me put it this way. Felicia poisons everything. Not even a pot plant is safe with her; she couldn't keep a freakin' weed alive. On Halloween she was three sheets to the wind, jingling her car keys," he says, shaking his head. "There was no way I was letting the kids get into the car with her."

"Was she often drunk?" asks Devil.

Carlos snorts. "Is the Pope Catholic?"

"Alcoholism is a disease, you know," says Susman. "It sounds like she needed help."

"That's putting it mildly," Carlos says, then checks his phone. He's had enough of the interview. "Are we going to be much longer? I need to call into a meeting at eleven."

"We'll have a quick look around if you don't mind."

There is a hesitation. They all know there is no search warrant.

"Sure," Amada says. "Knock yourself out."

De Villiers and Susman walk through the house slowly, their eyes trawling for details. Carlos stays outside, his foot bouncing in its running shoe. When they find a door to what looks like a basement, Susman takes a sharp inhalation and jiggles the handle. She gets that feeling of pressure on her chest. "It's locked," she whispers to De Villiers.

De Villiers gives the handle a forceful turn, but the door remains in place.

"Let me get that for you," says Carlos, from behind them, making them both jump. The pressure in Susman's chest gets tighter as her adrenaline spikes. She pictures Amada pushing them into the basement; imagines falling down the stairs and hitting her head, only to regain her consciousness and see Felicia in a cage. Her dry mouth tastes of stale coffee and bile. Armada pushes past her.

Robin swallows hard. "Why do you keep it locked?"

"Dangerous stuff down there," he says, grimacing as he turns the key. "Need to keep the kids out."

She realises she can't go down into the basement with him and looks at De Villiers, who reads her expression immediately.

"You stay up here," he tells her. Usually, she hates it when De Villiers tells her what to do, but this time she nods and lets him go. There is no fall down the stairs and no yelling from below. When he comes back up, he looks satisfied. "Let's go."

"It's his workshop," Devil tells her in the car.

"What kind of workshop?"

"Wood," says De Villiers, taking a corner in his slow and measured way. "Carpentry. It's his hobby."

"But why in the basement?"

De Villiers shrugs. "No space for it in the rest of the house."

"And it didn't feel weird down there?"

"You mean Fritzl-weird?"

"Yes. Or any kind of weird."

"Not that I could tell. I did swipe some wood shavings, though," he says and taps his jacket pocket. They didn't have a warrant, so they wouldn't be able to book it into forensics. Yet.

"You also get a feeling from him?" asked Susman. "A guilty feeling?"

"Ja," he says, looking at her. "He's hiding something."

The human condition, thinks Robin, as they exit the highway near the station.

"Susman!" says Blom, the tall Dutch detective. "What brings you to this hellhole of pestilence and plagues?"

Seko throws a scrunched-up piece of paper at him, which bounces off his chest. "Ignore the Flying Dutchman," says the sergeant. "He's learning advanced English and using big words to irritate us."

"I'm enlarging my vocabulary," says Blom.

"*Sies, man*," says Khaya. "Get a room."

"Susman's here for the Heddon case," says De Villiers.

"The boozer?" asks Blom.

"The missing woman," says Devil.

"Don't speak ill of the dead," says Khaya, and Blom looks suitably apologetic.

"See?" says Susman to De Villiers. "Everyone knows she's dead but you."

"What's wrong with being optimistic?" asks the captain.

"Optimism gets cops killed," says Susman. "Besides, it doesn't suit you."

They gravitate to De Villiers' office and perch amongst the piles of brown boxes.

"Did you nab the husband?" asks Blom.

"Ex-husband," says De Villiers.

"Not yet," says Susman.

"But it's him?"

"Probably." Susman stretches and sighs. "He admits to having an altercation with her on October 31st."

"Altercation," says Khaya. "There's a big word for you, Blom."

The Dutchman ignores the jibe. "But Heddon only went missing on the 5th of November."

"Correct," says De Villiers.

"Perhaps they met up and fought again," says Blom. "Or perhaps he didn't do it."

"Both are possible," says Susman. "It's a shame she didn't have any friends. I would have liked to ask them what her state of mind was after that argument."

"No need," says Khaya. "She was admitted to Park Lane hospital for alcohol poisoning on the 3rd of November. Looks like she was on a three-day bender and her liver didn't keep up with her."

"Maybe it was a bender. Maybe it was a cry for help. Or a suicide attempt."

"That would line up with her medical records," says Khaya, passing Susman a folder. "Bipolar, with severe depressive episodes. Refuses to take medication."

"Medication doesn't agree with everyone," says Susman.

De Villiers rubs his face. "Blow-up on the 31st. Hospitalised on the 3rd. Disappears on the 5th."

"Maybe she ran away," says Blom. "Or maybe she's lying dead in a ditch somewhere."

"Again, possible," says Susman.

The captain's phone rings. He answers and thanks the person on the other side of the line.

"Steenkamp is here," he says.

Robin and Devil walk into the interview room while Blom and Khaya watch from the other side of the two-way glass. The man stands up. He's young, brown-haired, and wearing spectacles. He's sweating.

"Glen Steenkamp?" asks De Villiers, and the man nods.

"You're the one who reported Felicia Heddon missing?" asks Robin, once they're all sitting down.

"Yes," he says, pale against the grey wall behind him. "Felicia misses work sometimes, and I cover for her. But this time it's been too long. I'm worried something has happened."

"What could have happened?"

"That's the thing about Felicia," says the young man. "Anything could happen."

"She has a drinking problem," says Devil.

A shadow of guilt winged over his face. Was it because he was in some way responsible, or was it because he didn't want to talk badly of Heddon behind her back?

"You were friends?" asks Robin.

"Colleagues," says Steenkamp. "As far as I could tell, Felicia didn't have many friends."

"You used to talk, though?"

"Not often," he says. "Only when she needed to. It was always about her."

"You thought she was selfish," says Susman.

Steenkamp shrugs. "No one's perfect."

"What do you think happened to her?" asks Robin.

He shrugs again and avoids eye contact. "I don't know."

"If you had to guess," says De Villiers.

Steenkamp stared at the wall a little longer. "I'd say ... I'd say her ex had something to do with it."

Susman sits up a little straighter. "Her ex? Carlos?"

"Ja," says Steenkamp. "They had an ... unhealthy relationship."

"Can you elaborate?"

"I don't know. It seemed twisted. Co-dependent. Toxic. That day she got hospitalised?"

"Yes?"

"He sent her something that morning. Something that made her go off the rails."

"What do you mean?"

"He couriered something to her house."

"What was it?"

"I don't know."

"How do you know this, if she wasn't at work?"

"The hospital phoned me when they admitted her for alcohol poisoning. Felicia had given my details for her emergency contact; I don't know why. I guess it was because I listened to her problems. She didn't have any friends, and she wouldn't have wanted her ex to know."

"So you visited her in the hospital?"

Steenkamp nods. "That's when she told me about the parcel from Carlos."

"You have no idea what it was?"

"No," says Steenkamp. "I was distracted. The doctor told me she almost died. That she needed to stop drinking or she *would* die. As if I was responsible for her."

"Did you feel responsible for her?" asks Robin.

"I didn't want to," says the young man. "But in a way, I guess I was."

Khaya finds the courier and waybill number. "I triangulated the date and address. A *bakkie* delivered a large parcel to Felicia at home, and she signed for it."

Devil grabs his jacket. "Let's go."

He drives a little faster than usual on the way to Felicia Heddon's house. They find the courier's packaging stuffed inside the garbage wheelie bin. A quick phone call to the courier company confirms it was sent from Carlos Amada.

"We need to know what was in the parcel," says Khaya, on the second call to the courier company. "I understand that," he says. "The warrant is on the way."

"Murder investigation," prompts Susman.

"It's evidence in a murder investigation," says Khaya.

"The press," she hisses.

"The press will be interested in the fact that your company was not willing to co-operate when a woman was missing."

De Villiers gives him a thumbs-up. Half an hour later, the sergeant is beaming. "Turns out the courier company doesn't like attention from the police," says Khaya, rubbing his ear.

"What does that mean?"

"They were raided by the drug squad a couple of years ago, found in possession of H."

"Heroin?"

"Affirmative. The company were cleared of all charges. They didn't know they were smuggling class A narcotics. But since then they've been passing their cargo through an X-ray machine, which takes photos of each item."

"Lucky for us," says Susman. "So, what was in the parcel that Amada sent Felicia?"

"Ready for this?" Khaya asks, and they all stare at him. He holds up his phone to show them the email attachment. It looks like a home-made coffin.

Devil stops. "Carlos Amada sent his ex-wife a freaking *coffin*?"

"That's messed up," says Khaya. Blom is speechless; his enlarged vocabulary has deserted him.

"Amada sends Felicia Heddon a coffin, and she goes missing the next day," says Robin. "Are you thinking what I'm thinking?"

"Surely not," says De Villiers, standing up and looking for his car keys.

"The neighbours heard that fight on Halloween," murmurs Blom. "I have them on record. The woman there said she heard Felicia say she was going to kill herself. Carlos yelled back to go ahead. Now we know he sent a coffin as a follow-up."

Khaya looks spooked. "When we checked out Heddon's house, there was a freshly planted bed in the back garden."

Susman frowns. "Amada said she couldn't keep a weed alive."

They stare at each other while the realisation sinks in.

"Blom," says De Villiers. "Send a team to Heddon's address. Tell them to bring shovels."

Susman's already walking to the car. "Let's go." They rush out of the station, and the wind slams the door behind them.

De Villiers and Susman arrive first, and they run around the side of the house. He kicks the side gate open that leads to the back garden, which is a field of yellowing grass interrupted only by a small patch of newly planted irises. Susman grabs a spade from the garage, and De Villiers takes it from her and slices into the soft earth with it. She looks for something else to dig with and settles for a rusted trowel. She gets on her knees and moves the soil as fast as she can, counting the days and hours in her head. How long had Felicia been buried? How long does it take someone to die when they are six feet under? Her knees go numb, and her muscles burn as she digs and digs. Soon the team arrives and takes over, letting De Villiers and Susman rest on the dying grass, muddy and out of breath. They don't look at each other; they watch as the men tunnel down and down till there's a thud and a shout, and more digging. They pry the lid off the coffin. Susman stays where she is, not wanting to peer inside the mess that was Felicia Heddon's mind.

"Not breathing," says one of the men. "No pulse."

De Villiers nods and gets a faraway look in his eyes. "Coffins don't bury themselves."

Felicia Heddon's nails are bloody and splintered; she had tried to escape. An empty bottle of vodka lies by her side.

"There is no sign of a struggle," the forensic assistant says. "Apart from her fingers, her body looks untouched."

Susman's mind whirrs. "It doesn't make sense."

"You know what else doesn't make sense?" says De Villiers. "We can't arrest Amada, because he has a rock-solid alibi. He was in Durban with his kids when Felicia was buried."

Susman's eyes glitter. "Steenkamp."

They blue-light to his place of work, and he doesn't resist arrest. He simply puts his hands up and says he's sorry. While they're interrogating him back at the station, Khaya knocks on the door.

"Positive match for DNA," he says, indicating Steenkamp. "Inside one of the gardening gloves."

"Why did you do it?" asks Robin. "Did she pay you?"

Steenkamp shakes his head. "She didn't have to. I was in love with her." His expression is one of surprise, as if it's the first time he's realised it. "Felicia was in so much pain. Her previous suicide attempts didn't work. I tried to talk her out of it, I swear. But she was desperate. She begged me."

"You buried her alive," says Susman.

"It's what she wanted. No one was supposed to find her."

"She tried to scratch her way out."

"That wasn't part of the plan. She promised me she was ready. She had tried so many times before. She was sure the coffin was the answer. She'd be out of pain, and Amada would be punished."

"It was murder," says De Villiers, but he doesn't sound convinced.

"It was mercy," says Steenkamp, his mouth turning down at the edges. He leans forward, resting his head on his arms, and begins to sob.

THE ICE SLIPPER

Written by the (fictional) MillenniarellaBot AI after being fed classic fairytales and feminist literature.

(Inspired by "The Christmas on Christmas" by Keaton Patti, who purportedly fed his bot thousands of Hallmark Christmas screenplays and then instructed him to write his own.)

Once upon a time, there was a girl named Cinder. She was as poor as a church mouse in a kingdom of atheists. Her mother was a pile of plague-stained bones, and her grieving father married a woman with a wire coat hanger for a heart, with which she would regularly beat Cinder. Her name was Lady Tremaine, and she was intensely jealous of her new daughter. Cinder's life was made more sour by the fact that she had two inherited sisters who treated her as if she were vermin virus lice pox.

"Don't wear that!" Anastasia would shout, emeralds flashing.

"Don't touch that!" Drizella would bellow, gold glittering.

"Don't eat that!" Lady Tremaine would yell, and smack Cinder's cheek with an ivory palm.

Cinder sewed her dresses from rags and owned no shoes. She looked like a feral pigeon amongst the strutting bejewelled peacocks. Her father looked at her sadly but blessed her with neither affection nor trinkets, for fear of the coat hanger heart.

When Cinder was a child, her mother used to say: "What doesn't kill you makes you stronger."

Then her mother died.

Point taken, Cinder had thought.

It was her life lesson always until she met her awful new sisters. Then she realised that horrible things happening to you do not, in fact, strengthen you. They fracture your soul until it sounds like ice cracking. They bend your mind and body downwards; a young hazel branch ready to snap.

When Anastasia put a rat in Cinder's bed to frighten her, Cinder stroked the creature and fed her the stale bread she had saved in her breakfast pocket. When Drizella put a rotten pumpkin in her chest of drawers, Cinder scooped out the maggoty churn and baked the shell in the sun. It turned into an elegant bowl, beautiful enough to rival the finest fall porcelain. When Lady Tremaine scraped Cinder's pale skin with a silver fork, leaving tine trails of blood along her legs, Cinder rubbed ash into the wounds to make them permanent lines. They were tattoos of her suffering; scars that mirrored how she felt on the inside.

One day the peacocks exploded in excitement when a gold carrier dove delivered an envelope. They opened it, and copper glitter snowed all around them; a glamorous blizzard.

"A ball!" shrieked Anastasia, her hair reaching for the ceiling, as if she had swallowed a power surge.

"A feast!" yelled Drizella, her tummy-jelly wobbling with an impromptu jig.

"A prince!" hissed coat-hanger-hearted Lady Tremaine, venomous desire blazing in her eyes.

Their cruel mother swept away the shrilling sisters to visit the most expensive dressmaker in town. They came back giggling and bustling with ribbons and feathers and gems. They instructed the cook to prepare only bone broth for breakfast, lunch and dinner to ensure the peacocks would fit into their new ballgowns. When Cinder expressed no interest in losing weight, they banished her from the table. She nicked some bread for herself and her pet rat, who she had named Suffragette, and who slept on her chest every night, protecting her from silver-tongued night terrors.

A white dove visited her dreams that night.

"You must go to the ball," cooed the bird. "It is the only way to smash the patriarchy."

"I have no desire to marry a prince," said Cinder.

"That is why you are perfect for the position," cooed the dream dove. "You must do it. It is the only way you will escape this prison you call home."

The next day, Cinder found an old ballgown of her late mother's and tried it on. The mirror was kind to her. She decided she'd go to the ball, and spent days sewing butterfly wings, dew diamonds, and blossom petals onto the dress.

When the evening of the ball arrived, Cinder swept downstairs in her beautiful gown. Envy turned them from peacocks to tigers. The three women took one look at Cinder and ripped the dress off her, tearing it to rainbow shreds.

"You're a servant," sneered Lady Tremaine. "Servants don't go to royal balls."

Cinder knew very well the invitation to the royal ball included her, as they had addressed it to all the maidens in the kingdom. "My chores are complete."

Anastasia smashed her wineglass on the floor. Drizella poured the cat's cream over the kitchen table. Lady Tremaine threw a thousand tiny dried lentils into the hearth.

"Once the house is clean," she said, "you may join us at the ball."

The peacocks sniggered and flounced from their home, toward the tittering golden palace. Cinder got down on her hands and knees and began picking up the lentils. What they left of her mother's dress became dusted with soot, and Cinder began to weep. The rat heard her crying and scuttled over, whiskers like soft silver needles. Cinder gathered the rodent into her arms and stroked her.

"Oh, Suffragette," she cried. "I wish I could go to the ball."

Some magic happened then; some alchemical combination of ash and salt and heartache—catalysed by the stroking of her skin on fur—for the dream dove appeared. It was sitting on the shoulder of a woman in white. The woman was lighting an ivory pipe, and the fragrant smoke curled in tendrils around her.

Cinder, still kneeling on the cold flagstone floor, looked up in awe, and held Suffragette closer.

"Right, darling," said the ghost, taking the pipe from her mouth. "Are you ready to smash the patriarchy?"

. . .

The white-robed ghost tidied the house with a flick of her wrist and then got to work on Cinder's appearance. She cleaned all the soot off her skin apart from her eyelids, which she left smoky. She stung Cinder's lips with baby bees and stained her nails with red lily pollen. The ghost whipped the rags and butterfly wings up from the floor, sewing them in mid-air with strands of spider silk. The result was a ball gown that shimmered and sparkled like nothing Cinder had ever seen. Using her beak, the dove piled Cinder's hair on top of her head and pinned it there with more diamonds and blossoms. They added to the outfit a pair of long satin gloves. The ghost flicked her hand at the pumpkin bowl, making it grow into a carriage, and Suffragette became a handsome horse.

Cinder clambered into the carriage, and it was only then when she realised she was barefoot.

The apparition moved her fingers in the direction of the water feature in the garden. It harnessed its fountain, making the water swirl around Cinder's delicate feet and freeze in the most beautiful design.

"Thank you for everything," said Cinder, sincerity forming a lump of coal in her throat.

"The magic will wear off at witching hour," warned the woman. "Make sure to get home before then."

The partygoers gasped when Cinder walked onto the dance floor, so exquisite and unusual was her dress. It seemed to have a life of its own. When the prince caught sight of her, he dropped the gloved hand of the maiden he was waltzing with and blinked violently, as if he had a splinter in his eye. He took Cinder's hand, and the couple danced all night, much to the disappointment of the other maidens. Cinder felt so happy and alive that she didn't realise how late it was, and when the palace tower clock struck midnight, she bolted from the ball. The prince, desperate not to lose her, gave chase, but she was faster than him. She left him with nothing but an ice slipper which began to melt in his hand.

Cinder's lone shoe turned to watery shards as she ran, and the dress fell away in pieces. Her long hair knotted and caught in a bramble bush, tearing it from her scalp. The pumpkin shell smashed to the ground and sliced her bare feet. Suffragette was nowhere to be seen. When the girl arrived home, she was dirty and in pain, and she fell asleep, shivering under the grey cloud sheets in her cold bed, missing Suffragette and wondering how dancing with Prince Charming would help to smash the patriarchy.

She woke with a start the next morning, wondering if it had all been a dream until she felt the stings and aches in her body.

"Get up!" yelled Lady Tremaine. "You're as lazy as a silkworm, but not as pretty. We're waiting for you to cook our breakfast."

Cinder swung herself out of bed and winced as her feet hit the floor. She limped into her servant rags. Her remaining hair was tangled, and she had eyes a raccoon would be envious of. The mirror was not kind to her. Usually, she would comb her hair; wash her face with a cold flannel, but she felt too hopeless and sad. Little did she know, Prince Charming had followed her trail of bloody footprints, bramble-hair, and a little rat named Suffragette, to find her house. There was a commotion at the door. Bugles and barking. Anastasia ripped a curtain off its rails.

"The prince!" she shouted. "He's come to get me!"

"Poppycock!" yelled Drizella. "He's here for me!"

Anastasia ran to answer, but Drizella tackled her to the floor. They crawled towards the door, elbowing and kicking one another, until Lady Tremaine ordered them back, straightened her dress, and allowed the royal party to enter the house. They all bowed as the prince bounced in.

"Please do excuse my intrusion," he said, his crown shining in the pink morning light. "But I have reason to believe my future queen lives under this roof."

Anastasia screamed in delight, and Drizella, fearing she would faint, grabbed a book to fan herself with. Lady Tremaine's cruel lips twisted into a smile. "How very wonderful," she said. "They are indeed special peacocks. Which one are you here for?"

"I'm not completely sure," said the prince, scratching his chin in an embarrassed way. "I felt blinded last night by the girl's beauty, and I can't seem to remember exactly what she looked like. She was as stunning as a branch of lightning; as sweet as new hay. I'm afraid she dazzled me to distraction."

An awkward silence settled on them like snow.

"This is Anastasia," said coat-hanger heart. "And this is Drizella." The daughters curtsied and fluttered their eyelashes at the handsome prince.

"Excellent. We'll start with Anastasia," said the prince and nodded at his footman.

"Er, you'll what?" asked the lady of the house, trying to keep the wrinkles from her brow.

The footman had with him a cold box, which he opened to reveal an ice slipper.

"May I?" the prince asked Anastasia, and she clutched her chest and nodded. She fell into the chair behind her and kicked off her shoes. The prince kneeled before her, and Lady Tremaine gasped, perhaps thinking of the genuine chance her daughter had of being married into royalty. Anastasia pulled and pushed and huffed and puffed, but no matter how she squirmed, she could not get her foot to squeeze into the small frozen slipper. Next up was Drizella, but Lady Tremaine quickly whisked her into the garden and cut off her toes with her pruning shears, bandaging them up with black socks. Drizella's wounded feet fitted into the slipper, and the lady celebrated, but then the blood leaked from the sock and melted the frosty shoe.

The prince became angry. "I should lock you up in the castle dungeon for trying to deceive me, but I will take pity on you instead. Live in freedom, but may the guilt of your actions keep you in a cage forever."

"Your love for the people and your mercy is unrivalled," said the footman with cartoon hearts in his eyes. He bowed. They all stared at the puddle of toe blood on the floor as it ran together with the ice water. Cinder rushed in to clean it up.

"And who might you be?" asked the prince, surprised at the visage of a girl with wild hair. When she looked up at him, he instantly recognised her smoky eyes.

"It's you," he said, mouth agape. "It's you! You're the one who wore the ice slippers without them melting."

"She is clearly a witch," said the footman. "We should burn her at once."

(That is when Cinder understood why she needed to smash the patriarchy.)

"Codswallop," said the prince. "This beauty is no sorceress. She will be my queen."

The wedding was a grand affair. The castle was a snow globe of glitter, beribboned with bunting the colour of duck eggs. The royal tailor fabricated an exquisite dress to match what Cinder had been wearing the night Prince Charming had met her. The white dove carried the gown's train, holding the gossamer ribbons in her beak. The feast was a delicious montage of flavours served on spinning plates. The only hiccup was when the dove swooped down to pluck the eyes from the uninvited Anastasia and Drizella, who had sneaked in through the back door to poison the wedding food. Without their eyes, they couldn't find the vat of boiling soup, and the poison stayed in their blood-soaked pockets, much to Lady Tremaine's outrage. Prince Charming's parents, the king and queen, welcomed Cinder into the family and gave her gifts of silk, tanzanite, and silver oyster pearls.

When they died, quite mysteriously, together in their bed one night after dinner, the prince was called to his royal duty, and after the coronation ceremony, King Henry and Queen Cinder took their thrones. This seemed like a Happily Ever After, but with the late royals rolling in their graves, Cinder lost her happiness. Her new husband, without the guidance of his parents, did what he pleased, including hunting wild birds and foxes with his footman and cutting down magnificent oak trees to extend the kingdom. Suffragette told Cinder of all the homeless squirrels and hapless mice losing their shelter to the King's zealous ambition. When Cinder told her husband it made her unhappy, he replied with "You are a jewel. You're too beautiful to worry about things like this."

He wanted Cinder to mind her manners and her dress, and to focus on her wifely duties, especially those involved in producing an heir. Cinder couldn't help remembering her promise to the ghostly woman in white who had made her the ice slippers, and she watched in disdain as the new king grew fat and beet-cheeked from his excesses.

"I'm building a wall," growled the king one night at dinner, his lips and teeth black from too much merlot.

"A wall?" asked Cinder. "Whatever for?"

"To keep the gypsies out," he replied.

"I'd prefer if you didn't," said Cinder. "The castle grounds are wonderful as they are, and the gypsies are good people."

"You don't understand these things," said the king. "It is not a woman's worry."

"Indeed, it is my worry," said Cinder. "You have already cut down centuries of trees, and I cry for the foxes."

The king laughed. "Your tears, though salty, are wasted. You will come hunting with me tomorrow and see what sport it is."

"No," said Cinder. "I shall not."

"You shall," said the king, and left the dining room with the words hanging in the air like angry butterflies.

"Oh, Suffragette," whispered Cinder to the rat in her pocket. "Whatever shall I do?"

The dream dove appeared at the window, tapping in morse code on the glazing.

The next morning was cold, and Cinder's breath plumed from her mouth like the memory of the pipe-smoke of the white-robed ghost woman. Cinder dressed in her jodhpurs and boots, ready to ride with the king. The footman gave her a weapon: a smart, oil-black rifle. Cinder hung it snugly across her chest instead of the baby she was supposed to be cradling; the heir she had not yet conceived despite the king's best efforts. The king arrived and was happy to see his queen. Once they were both in the saddle, he leant over and tapped her knee in approval, and it felt to Cinder like a hornet sting.

They rode out to the soundtrack of bugles and bullets, and Cinder loved the feeling of the nimble horse galloping beneath her, and the chilled morning wind in her hair. The king shot five pheasants before

Cinder had once discharged her rifle. The king and queen were alone in the dark wood together when they spotted a fox.

"Now's your chance," he whispered, pointing at the red-breasted animal.

Cinder shook her head. The horse beneath her trembled.

"Shoot it!" he hissed.

Cinder raised the rifle and watched the creature through her scope. It was a beautiful maroon vixen with inky eyes.

"Shoot it!" the king fizzed, and when Cinder wouldn't, he lost patience and raised his own rifle, firing it before the queen could alert the animal. The crack of the king's gun was like a hard slap on Cinder's cheek, reminding her of how Lady Tremaine used to strike her. Cinder dismounted and ran towards the fox, picking up the leaking vulpine corpse.

The dream dove cooed, and the ghost woman in white robes appeared in the forest. It was only then that Cinder realised the woman was the ghost of her late mother.

You know what to do.

There was only one way Cinder could stop the destruction of the land by the king; stop the cruel hunting and the building of the wall. Stop the felling of trees, and plant more instead. The only way it would happen is if she ruled over the kingdom, not as a pretty ornament, a jewel accessory, but as the sole sovereign. The dead fox in her hands painted them red. She gently wound the vixen's body over her shoulders—a bloody shawl she'd always wear to remind herself of this moment—raised her rifle and shot the king in the heart. He gasped and slumped over, and his spooked horse galloped away, never to be seen again. Queen Cinder tightened the fox shawl around her neck and began walking back to her castle.

4

THE FERTILITY CAVE

AUTHOR'S NOTE:

This is an adapted excerpt of 'The Underachieving Ovary' — a (very!) personal memoir I wrote about my struggle to conceive.

~

UNZIPPED

It's been ten months since I binned the blister pack that used to contain my contraceptive pill. My gynaecologist, who I call the BFG, wants me to go for some tests.

'So, about your devil womb,' the Big Friendly Giant said in his Dutch accent (but not in so many words), "it's freaky, and we're going to need to check it out." Okay, he didn't really say that.

'Because you have a scary-as-hell double-horn, we need to make sure you don't have weirdo double-anything-else, you organ-doppelgänger.'

He didn't say that either, but you get the idea.

59

The bicornuate uterus scenario is a congenital thing: it happens while you are a developing foetus. Usually when you need two of something (like lungs) your cells form things that split *et voila!* One becomes two. Sometimes it works the other way around, and two things will merge to create one. As with any stage of development, if there is some kind of genetic accident or a biological glitch, things can go wrong. In my case, the BFG says that the pair of things meant to knit together to form my uterus only got 60% of the job done, hence the top of my uterus being ... un-knitted. Only halfway zipped. The case being such, who knows what else was melded / not melded enough / doubled up like cheap gin on a discount cruise? We'll need to have a proper look-see.

~

THEY TIE HER DOWN

That was the worst experience ever.

It was like being in a medically-themed horror movie. You know the ones. Rusty equipment, maniacal doctors, needles the size of toothpicks. It was terrifying.

Picture this: Open on young, fresh-faced girl (in jeans and a cheap and cheerful cereal-themed shirt from Thailand) showing up at a nice-enough hospital. Waiting and waiting and filling out reams of medical forms, while thinking of the work she is missing: she runs her own business and every lost hour counts. She thinks of the emails bottle-necking in her inbox, the deliverymen of urgent orders ringing the doorbell of her empty house. She is then presented with the estimated costs of the procedures she is to undergo and almost faints. She doesn't know if her medical aid will cover it. Medical aids are assholes when it comes to that, even though infertility is a disease recognised by the WHO.

Eventually, she is given a backless hospital gown the colour of well-chewed gum and told to strip. She isn't allowed to wear undies or her engagement ring. She's taken to a room where she lies on a cold stainless steel table, next to a tray holding a giant syringe on a hospital-blue napkin. Above her is a vast X-ray machine that looks a hundred years old. Despite the metal table leaching the warmth from her back and making it ache, she starts perspiring. They tie her down.

'The restraints are so that you don't move while the machine is taking pictures,' says the smiley young nurse.

The radiologist walks in, wearing a curt expression and her customary radiation-proof armour.

'We're going to inject you with iodine,' she says as if that is a perfectly polite thing to do. 'The X-ray will pick up the iodine in your bloodstream and show us its passage – show us your renal system – to see if there is a problem there.'

The BFG had explained that the biggest concern is that I have either only one kidney or two sets of two. Four kidneys, I reckoned, was a bonus. No wonder I could keep up drinking beer with the boys. Four kidneys! Maybe I could sell some to pay for this X-ray. One kidney, on the other hand, would not be so lucky. How funny that I just assumed that I had two to begin with. Brainwashed by biology lessons. How many do I really have? Bets, anyone? It could be like a game if this room weren't so damn scary.

After the iodine is pushed into the sweat-soaked girl's body, the horror film takes on a comedic slant, as all good/bad horror movies do. To work the ancient machine, the nurse has to run from one side of the room to the other, dragging the bulky ceiling-mounted contraption along with her while it shudders on its rails, threatening to fall off and crush all three of the people beneath it. Bang! Bang! Bang! Bang! it goes on every passage. Underneath the banging is a whirring, a clicking, as the X-ray film is exposed.

'Again,' says the radiologist. Again, again, again. Banging and clicking and whirring until the nurse is out of breath from running and dragging and still the radiologist wants more, adjusting my pose in between.

'Again,' she says, relentless, some kind of insane perfectionist.

'These pictures aren't for the fucking World Press Photo awards,' the patient doesn't say out loud. She looks at the other women in the room, protected by their heavy aprons. Thinks that this massive dose of radiation can't be good for her organs, either. What does a radiologist know about fertility? And with fertility at stake, who cares, anyway, about an extra kidney either way? She imagines the rays bombarding her ovaries, zapping her eggs by the thousands. Microwaving her baby-maker. Wouldn't it be terrible, she thinks, if the very first procedure she undergoes to get pregnant actually renders her forever infertile? She sweats some more.

~

MIKE JUNIOR

We call our unborn (or, more correctly, un-conceived) baby 'Mike Jnr'. It's shorthand for our (nowadays brittle) dream of having a baby. It helps to have a name. It makes him seem more real, less of a fantasy. It also helps in writing email updates to friends and family — keeps it light. Subject: 'Update on Mike Jnr!' instead of: 'Feeling poor, sad and hopeless. Send schedule 16 painkillers.'

I've always written my goals in the sand. Before I started my business, when I was 'stuck' in advertising, I used to write 'Pulp Books' in the wet sea sand. Before that, it was 'Mike'. Now I write 'Mike Jnr' at every opportunity I get. It's my way of committing it to the universe, making the wish more tangible. Mike calls it 'collapsing the possibility'.

It's been 18 months of writing it in the sand, and now I am less particular about where I scribble his name: steamed up mirrors, books, chalkboards, paper notes that get buried in the garden. I commit it over and over again to the earth. It may seem silly, but I feel that it has a certain power.

∽

THE FERTILITY CAVE

Mandie and Avish weren't sure what to get me for my birthday. They knew all I wanted was a baby, so they got creative. (No, they didn't kidnap a newborn, although they assure me that they did consider it.)

Instead, they organised and sponsored a weekend away in Clarens for Mike and I. A weekend dedicated to conceiving. Not (necessarily) a dirty weekend, but to visit the fertility cave there. How they even knew about the cave, I can't guess. Mandie is on every contraceptive known to man and mammal. She was conceived while her mother was on the pill, so she takes no chances. While she is really good with babies, if you ask her if she wants one she slaps you with a glare that would freeze lava.

So last night we packed our bags and headed out to the Free State. I would never say no to a weekend away, and Clarens is so beautiful with its golden mountains, but I don't hold much hope for a miracle from some dirty cave that (I'm guessing) someone once thought looked like a giant vagina.

But we have gone from 'Not Trying' to 'Trying Absolutely Everything', and if that includes a punani grotto, then I'm in. My only objective this weekend is to have fun, and an open mind.

...

The pilgrimage didn't start well. It's not that the cave isn't well signposted, it's not signposted AT ALL. We drove around with no clue where we were going, and I couldn't help feeling that it was a cruel and apt metaphor for our fertility journey so far.

At first, I couldn't bear to ask someone. I was sure no one would know, anyway. But we were about to give up, and I couldn't go back to Jo'burg without having visited the cave. The first few people regarded us with confusion, and vague suspicion, (*Fertili-what-what?*) But eventually someone knew what we were talking about and pointed us in the right direction.

We finally found a little sand road that we had missed the first 23 times we had driven past. We picked up some pedestrians who we bribed to show us the way. I was worried they may be axe-murderers, leading us to a dead-end to rob us of our meagre possessions. The trip included going through a gate that warned you to not enter. We were, like, 'Are you sure this is right?' and the guys were like, 'Yes!' and we were, like, 'We are so going to get axed.'

We pulled into a makeshift parking lot in the middle of a huge herd of sheep. There were two or three cars, but not a cave or another person in sight. We watched the sheep for a while, not sure what to do, when we saw people walk past us, making their way up the hill. That's when we realised that we would be working hard for our little bit of fertility magic: we had to hike to get to the cave.

I don't know what I was expecting. Perhaps something like the virility cave we saw in Thailand: a short, easy walk on a beach and *voila!* a huge cavern full of phallic symbols. You giggle and admire them while someone chops open a coconut cocktail for you.

The hike was long and steep, and we weren't dressed for it, so we were hot and a bit grumpy on our way up. I was surprised at how many people were also walking the path. They were dressed in church gear and carried staffs, so we guessed the caves held more enchantment than just of the fertility variety.

Eventually, we reached the top and hopscotched over a river to get to the cave, and it was as though we had crossed into another world. It wasn't as much a cave as it was a hobbit warren. Built into the recesses were tiny interconnected dwellings with small hobbit-sized doors (I kept my eyes peeled for hobbits, but no such luck). Instead, ordinary-looking humans were walking around, among goats, dogs, cats and chickens. The closest thing I could find to a hobbit was a sweet little boy, about 3 years old, with an easy smile and dusty feet. He followed us, pointing things out. He let me pick him up and carry him while we explored. His parents didn't seem to be around, and I briefly considered taking him home with us, day-dreamed about looking after him. Then I remembered that kidnapping was illegal. If getting pregnant outside jail was this tricky, the chances of it happening while locked up might be even trickier. It would take a lot of planning to get Mike to pay a conjugal visit at precisely the right time of the month.

'Warden, please, I have to see my husband right now. Like, right now. In the next hour at the latest.'

(I facepalm myself for not thinking ahead and ordering KFC for her lunch today).

'Er, no. Get back to pulling out those blackjacks.'

'You don't understand. It's my window. (Whispers:) My ovulation window.'

(Warden slaps some sense into me.)

'Blackjacks!'

The hobbit houses were immaculate and swept to within an inch of their lives. This wasn't some kind of (inconvenient) place to squat; it was clearly revered as some kind of holy place. There was a shrine, oily with years of molten wax, where we said a quick Hail-Mary or some-such. I've never been good with religion or bowing to man-made edifices, but I was wearing my Open Mind. After looking around in fascination and petting the odd smelly goat, we were shown to the Fertility Lady's place. She made us wait outside while she did what I guessed was some preparatory voodoo.

When she was ready for us, she called us in. We're not the shortest couple: we had to make ourselves hobbit-sized by folding ourselves in half and crawling in. It was clearly a place of miracles: the fact that we all fitted into such a tiny space was a special kind of sorcery.

The interior was dim, cramped, and completely pimped. An array of fertility icons gleamed in the candlelight. The lady started off by chanting and dusting me (with what I guess was a feather duster with special powers and not a regular one from the local Shoprite/Checkers) and singing a bit. Then she put her hands on my stomach and pressed quite hard. Mike and I couldn't look at each other, afraid to offend her by laughing. She picked up a silver-framed picture of a (white) mother nursing a baby. I wondered if only white people came to ask her for help. She cradled the frame like an infant, rocking it, and kissed it, then passed it to me to do the same, making kissy noises. I cradled it, and it made me feel like I was a child again, playing in a (uniquely eccentric) friend's dollhouse.

Next came the really fun part: She produced an old, scratched plastic bottle (Sprite? Stoney?) filled with dirty water. Mike looked worried, but I wasn't nervous. I thought she might sprinkle it around us, like holy water. Holy Fertility Cave Water. But it turned out that Mike had good reason to be twitchy. She poured some out into an enamel mug and passed it to me, motioning for me to drink it. I thanked her and pretended to take a sip, making sure my lips weren't anywhere near the filthy stuff, but she had clearly seen this trick before and got really bossy about me drinking it all. I looked for somewhere I could tip it out, but the place was so tiny, and she was staring right at me so there was no way I wouldn't be busted. At her insistence, I took a sip (I know! Hepatitis C. Cholera. There would be no getting pregnant now. But what choice did I have?). It was ice cold and tasted of sand and candle wax. I shudder to think of where it came from and was sure that I'd be rolling around in agony with some kind of vicious stomach bug that night. I was suddenly convinced that this woman wanted me to puke all my evil infertile guts out. And I had fallen for it! Dammit!

Fortunately (for me) she then turned her attention to Mike. She took some of the freezing water and, wait for it, POURED IT INTO HIS EAR. He wasn't expecting it (obviously), and certainly wasn't expecting it to be so damn cold, and he screamed. A proper scream that reverberated on the close clay walls. Oh my God, I laughed so much I almost wet my shorts. I laughed and laughed. I was practically hysterical. Trying to not laugh made me laugh more. He tried to shake the water out of his eustachian tube (this is where his surfing experience should have come in handy), but the magic (read: filthy) water was there to stay. After all the commotion she still wanted to pour water in his other ear. And he let her. And he screamed again. I was finished.

Then it was my turn again, giving Mike a moment to shake and smack his head like someone deranged. She gave me the whole bottle of water, told me to drink it all (thankfully not right there and then, but rather as homework) and then put a shiny plastic tiara on my head. I will never forget that picture in my mind of Mike trying to get the water out of his ears and me, in a tiara, cuddling and kissing a picture of some stranger's baby, trying to stifle my maniacal laughing. If it had happened anywhere else, I'm sure we would have been given strait-jackets and our own padded cells.

At last, we were let out into the sunshine, and we scrabbled in our pockets for cash. We weren't expecting an actual person or ritual, just an old cave, so we didn't bring our wallets on the hike. We only had a couple of notes and coins (certainly not enough for a miracle, we were sure) and handed them over sheepishly. I think she had expected more, explaining that the money was for 'the angels', but we didn't have anything else to give.

The little boy had waited outside for us and was happy to see us again, but when he realised we were going home, he started crying. We both gave him a hug and told him not to cry, which made him cry more.

We said goodbye and ran down the hill, our spirits high from all the strangeness and laughing. We passed a *bliksem*-drunk man on his way up, tried to give him a wide berth, but that didn't stop him from shouting some slurry profanities in our direction. Nothing like a dirty drunk to bring you back down to earth.

In the car, Mike was, like, 'I can't believe you drank that siff water.'

I was, like, 'Me neither!'

'That was not a good idea.'

'I think I've got Hepatitis.'

'You'll be lucky if that's all you've got,' he said, and I agreed, and we laughed some more as we tried not to run over any sheep on our way out.

~

NO CRYING OVER BAD EGGS

I had some more blood tests done. I thought that even though the rest of my fertility was trash, I hadn't yet heard anything TOO bad about my eggs, and happily (naïvely) assumed that they were A-okay. Or at least okay enough to be able to conceive. Dr G had other ideas.

'Look, guys, there is no delicate way to say this.'

'Spit it out, doc, we can handle it. Probably heard worse.'

'You're old.'

'We're not old! We're thirty-one! That's like the new twenty! We're still shiny!'

'You're old on the inside. Not shiny on the inside. Old and shrivelled.'

'That's a bit harsh.'

'Have you *seen* the state of your babymaker? I have. And it's Not Pretty.'

'Wow, feel free not to sugar-coat the truth.'

'We don't have time for sugar. We don't know how long you have before your endo comes back. Plus, your eggs are running out. They're not great eggs by any stretch of the imagination, but at least while you've still got some, we've still got something to work with.'

My baby cannon cringes. She's had enough of the barrage of insults. No wonder she is feeling hollow-cheeked.

So my eggs, apart from being rare, are past their sell-by date. Not a good combination. It's not the end of the world, it just means that whatever we plan to do, we need to do it as quickly as possible. There is no time to cry over bad eggs. There's been plenty of crying over dodgy uteri and tangled up nether-organs: no more tears now. It's time for action. Every month that passes literally lowers our chances. He recommends three timed cycles starting now (a month after the surgery). I've a had a bit of a spring-clean down there and a septum snip, so there's a chance they'll work. If they don't, we'll go straight to IVF.

Without even discussing it between ourselves, Mike and I both nodded decisively at the doc. All the conversations we have had about reasons not to do IVF from our collective memories. Yes, we nodded, let's get on with this thing.

'Okay,' we agreed, 'we don't want to wait too long.'

Dr G looked at us. 'You're here because you already waited too long.'

BABIES EVERYWHERE

I'm feeling better about everything, actually. I've had the surgeries, I'm all cleaned up Down There, I'm definitely going to ovulate, and I have an amazingly good-looking sperm donor on hand. This might be the month I fall pregnant. I know, I know, it's a long shot, but there is a chance. Every day this month is brightened by that glimmer.

Have you ever seen the Starbucks espresso ads? They won an award at Cannes a while back. I cannot watch them without laughing. Something about the over-the-top humour appeals so much to me.

I love the 'Glen' (Eye of the Tiger) execution. My favourite is the one in the open-plan office where everyone is entirely hopped up on caffeine. Hilarious! My copywriter at Jupiter used to joke that I was like the broody female character (crazy-eyed: "Babies Everywhere!" she shouts, while stuffing her cardigan full of office supplies, to look pregnant.) He used to act it out in our office, and we'd piss ourselves. I loved working with him, he'd always make me laugh. He did especially good impersonations of Doctor Evil from Austin Powers. We did some good work together and were very close. "Babies Everywhere!"

All of which reminds me of one of his (many) pearls of infinite wisdom, which has stood me in good stead:

"If you don't laugh, you cry." — Stephen Anderson

The humiliation continues. Part of this first medicated cycle is to have a PCT: Post-coital test. This does not involve, as you may think, a pub-like pop quiz after a good shag. Instead, we are to 'do our homework' during our ovulation window, and go to the clinic first thing the next morning (without showering) to witness how Mike's swimmers are faring up the creek.

Apparently, there is such a thing as 'hostile cervical mucus'. It means that the cervical environment is acidic and, as you can guess, not suitable for sperm.

A test! I feel completely unprepared. Should I be eating more yoghurt or something?

~

TMI: PROJECT DOUCHE

I'm going to go out tonight to drink a vast amount of whisky. Okay, I'm in the middle of a medicated cycle so I'll just have one and make my friends do the rest of the drinking for me. As you have probably gathered, the PCT did not go well. In fact, it couldn't have gone any worse.

So we're there in the room at the clinic, blinking weary eyes, so early that neither of us has even registered that it's morning. The doc takes a swab and smears it on the little glass slide and puts it under the microscope, which shows us what is happening on the big screen adjacent to it. That woke me up.

I think my jaw hung open for a while, as Dr G sort of gathered himself and started talking. I didn't hear anything for those first few minutes. My attention was wholly focused on the massacre before my eyes: all I could see were hundreds of dead or dying sperm. The fallen soldiers were one thing — ghost-sperm! — but watching the others writhe and struggle and swim in wounded circles was just too much. And I was the one who had maimed and killed them. I could almost hear them groaning in agony. In my imagination, one particularly brave tadpole, shivering at the beginning of his death throes, urges the rest of his squad to go on without him.

I've said it before, I'll say it again. WTF.

I had given the poor things an acid bath — they never stood a chance.

'Never' being the operative word that makes this difficult to accept: Of all the months of 'not trying,' followed by the months of 'really trying': taking my temperature, prodding my body for signals, the carefully-timed ovulation-window sex ... of all those months (18 failed cycles), all that hope that was dashed, over and over again, and all that pain, and actually, there had never been a chance. THERE HAD NEVER BEEN A CHANCE.

I feel like I've been swiped sideways. I feel like (emotionally-speaking) I was walking down the street, perfectly alive, and some asshole in a BMW skipped a stop sign and sent me flying. Irrationally, I felt the need to apologise to Mike. I thought that if someone had killed thousands upon thousands of *my* soldiers, I would at least expect a card and a fruit basket.

'Wow,' I said when I finally regained my ability to speak. 'That's not good.'

I expected Dr G to don a hazmat suit and usher me out of his building. It was clear that I was radioactive and a hazard to the general population.

I expected him to say: 'Holy Moses! I've never seen such a gruesome slaughter. Who would have guessed that a seemingly benevolent vagina could be responsible for such annihilation?' and then: 'Would you mind if we took you and your cervical environment along to our next PCT WTAF conference? I'm sure the fraternity will find your mucus entirely fascinating.'

Instead, he recommended I douche with bicarb. I was, like, do what with what-what? I have never douched in my life. I thought douching had gone the way of trepanning and toothbrush moustaches. I thought the last people to douche were promiscuous French women in the 1800s. I thought only people with a severe form of OCD would even consider douching nowadays; it's an old wives tale that I have absolutely no interest in trying. He said the alkalinity of the bicarb should neutralise the acidity of the CM, creating a less hazardous playground for the swimmers. Those poor guys. I don't want to be the fertility version of Idi Amin. It looks like I have no choice but to try it.

Project Douche

Tools required:

1x (larger-than-expected) douching instrument (syringe with bulb) (Strange-looking thing - I think I may have gasped when the nurse whipped it out of her supplies cupboard. I was, like, Holy Moly! What the hell is that thing?)

1x warm bath

1x box of bicarbonate of soda (or, in Afrikaans, Koeksoda! Koek, get it? Hee.)

1x teaspoon

1x glass beer tankard that you will never drink out of again. Not because it goes anywhere near your — ahem — hostile mucus, but because every time you see it, you will be reminded of the not-romantic exercise of irrigating your punani.

Also handy: supreme gymnastic talent, or, lacking that, a highly developed sense of humour.

. . .

Method:

1. Run a shallow bath. Not too hot. Hot baths are bad for fertility. Don't you know anything?!

2. Mix one heaped teaspoon of bicarb with one tankard of warm water. Don't be distracted by the logo on the flask. This is not the time to think about having a nice cold beer.

3. Get in the bath.

4. Use the bulb syringe to suck up bicarb solution from the tankard.

5. Kind of angle yourself backwards, on your haunches, while simultaneously holding on for dear life and squirting the solution up your nethers. This requires a reasonable amount of dexterity and determination.

6. Relax, and let it out.

7. Repeat steps 5 and 6 as many times as you need to, to finish the solution, trying to not pull any muscles or slip and brain yourself on porcelain.

8. While practising your unique form of douche-yoga, accidentally knock over the box of bicarb so that it lands in a puddle of spilt bathwater. Swear a little. Crave a cigarette, even though you haven't smoked in five years.

9. Try again. In the middle of a particularly challenging pose, you hear footsteps outside the bathroom. As if caught in a lewd act, you immediately drop everything and start whistling.

10. When your husband comes in, you sit on the bulb syringe to hide it and pretend to drink the bicarb solution out of the tankard.

11. 'Staying hydrated!' you shout at him, in case he doesn't buy it. You add an enthusiastic thumbs-up and smile with all your teeth.

12. He looks at you as if you are insane. There is a little fear in his eyes. He backs out of the bathroom door, perhaps even the front door, grabbing his toothbrush and sleep shorts on his way.

13. When it is over, lie back in the cold, quimmy water and wonder what the hell your life has come to. A pre-sexy-time bath used to consist of a glass of red wine, baby oil, and scented candles. Stare at the brightly-lit bulb syringe and feel suitably depressed.

14. Now snap out of it! Time to feel sexy! Forget that you just used a common baking ingredient to neutralise your acid bath of a vagina, and hope that your husband decided to stick around.

15. Hubba-hubba, bow-chick-a-wow-wow, etc.

～

SAVING PRIVATE RYAN (with apologies to Robert Rodat)

Another PCT today. (Waking up when it's still dark to sit in traffic to come to a clinic to wait in a waiting room to have your babymaker swabbed and then put under a microscope is so awesome.)

I watched the screen through my fingers, not being able to take another battleground scene — I sense that the first one will forever haunt me, to the soundtrack of 'Saving Private Ryan' — but yay for old wives tales and bulb syringes: the swimmers were alive! I felt like high-fiving my cervix.

～

ANGRY VAGINAS AND SANGRIA

. . .

Mike has taken to calling my CM 'The Hostiles' (from the TV series 'Lost').

So now, douching has become 'taking out The Hostiles'. Sometimes, during sex, I picture a tribe of creepy island survivors camping out on the dirty upside-down hill of my cervix. It's them against The Swimmers.

My female friends and I refer to hostile cervical mucous as 'Angry Vagina'. The first time I heard the phrase, I spat sangria out of my nose.

'I also have an Angry Vagina!' says an acquaintance at a party, chinking my glass of wine. Forget the First Wives Club, we're the Angry Vaginas. And there are a lot of us. Does naturally sperm-friendly CM even exist? we wonder out loud to each other in some-one's kitchen at a party. If it does, I bet it's as rare and difficult to harness as a unicorn's fart.

I referred to my Angry Vagina the other day in company not yet familiar with the term, and she sprayed her drink out of her nose, too.

Nose-irrigation: the initiation ceremony for Angry Vaginas all over the world.

Then I told her about my visit to the Fertility Cave and Mike shrieking when the witchdoctor poured freezing water into his ear. I had to pour her a new gin and tonic.

5

THROW HER TO THE WOLVES

"THROW HER TO THE WOLVES" was originally written as a radio play.

~

The grey-haired headmistress kept her voice low. "Is it essential to keep the pupils here? What kind of questions do you have? Who do you need to speak to?"

"We don't know yet," said detective Seko.

"Let's talk in my office," Grashawn says, already striding in that direction. "Miss Simpson, you come, too."

The young woman looked startled. "Me?"

Headmistress Grashawn stopped. "Has no one told you?"

"Er—"

"She's in your homeroom," said the headmistress. "Jessica Steyn. The poor girl Mr Damster found—"

The woman began to wring her hands. "Oh, dear. I didn't know."

"It's why we need you as a temp today. The class's regular teacher couldn't handle coming in. Thank goodness for your agency; I'd be stuck without them."

"Not the easiest way to start your first day at Wolverhampton," said the detective, and Angela Simpson gave him a tight smile. They reached the headmistress's office and spilled inside, closing the door behind them.

"Please," said Grashawn. "Have a seat."

"Thank you, headmistress," said detective Seko.

Grashawn looked amused, despite the dread that painted her face pale. "You don't have to call me headmistress."

"Sorry," said the detective. "It comes naturally to me. I also went to a boarding school like this. Well, not quite like this—"

"Of course," said the headmistress.

"Our school certainly wasn't the top school in the province," he continued.

"In the country," murmured Miss Simpson.

The detective looked at the fidgeting teacher. "Sorry?"

"Wolverhampton High School for Girls is the top-performing school in the country. Well, it used to be, anyway, until this—"

They were all jolted by the sudden loud ringing of the telephone on Grashawn's desk. She reached over and cancelled the call.

"Mrs Grashawn," said Seko. "Jessica Steyn was your top swimmer, correct?"

The phone rang again, and she cut off the sound with a stab of her large-knuckled finger. "Damn press," she muttered. "They're like barracudas at a sardine run."

It immediately rang again, and Grashawn whipped the line out, leaving the three of them in silence. Detective Seko cleared his throat. "That's what her father kept saying. That Jessica was such a strong swimmer, that she'd earned her national colours three years in a row. They had high hopes for the Olympic team."

"Yes," said the headmistress. "She was the best swimmer we've ever had. We were very proud of her. That's why she was in the pool enclosure. It's out of bounds—and locked—for pupils from 6 pm till 6 am, but we had a special arrangement with her. She had her own key so she could train at any time."

"You will have a lawsuit on your hands," said Seko. "Did her parents know?"

"Mr Steyn was the one who requested the key."

Angela Simpson walked into her new classroom, which sounded live a nest of wasps. When the teenage girls saw her, they hushed.

"Morning, ladies," she said, leaning against her desk to appear less nervous than she was. "I'm Miss Simpson, and I'll be your temporary homeroom teacher until Mrs Siceka feels well enough to return." The girls stared at her. "Will you please all go to your desks?"

The students find their chairs and scrape them on the floor as they sit. "I realise how shocked and upset you must be. If you look at the board, you'll see that my phone number is there. I want you to feel free to call me at any time. If you need to talk, if you want to tell me something, if you ever need help." She looked at the sea of traumatised faces before her. "Now, usually I'd ask you all to stand up and introduce yourselves so I can learn your names, but given the situation—"

"It's a good idea, Miss Simpson," said a pretty blond girl wearing a highly decorated Head Girl blazer. "It may take our minds off it for a while. I'm sure we'll all be allowed to go home soon, anyway." The other girls murmured their assent.

Miss Simpson took a deep breath. "All right, then. I recognise you from the assembly this morning. You're the Head Girl?

"Yes, ma'am. My name is Candice. Candice Compton."

"Thank you, Candice. Next?"

"I'm Wandi," announced the next girl. "Wandi, as in, wonderful." There are snorts of laughter.

The next girl stood up. "Terry. Short for Theresa."

"Like Mother Theresa," said Miss Simpson.

"Hardly," Wandi snarked under her breath.

"Next?"

Terry didn't sit down. "What about you?"

Angela Simpson's cheeks warmed a little. "Me?"

"Which school are you from? Why did you leave? Are you married?" There was some tittering, and then silence as they waited for her to answer.

She turned away to hide the colour in her cheeks. "I think we'll leave that story for another day." Simpson finally found the button, and the whiteboard reeled slowly down behind her. "I'll get the hang of everything soon, I hope—"

The class gasped.

"What?" asked Miss Simpson. "What's wrong?"

"Behind you," said Candice, wide-eyed.

Miss Simpson turned to look at the whiteboard, and her hands flew up to her mouth. "Oh! Oh dear! Who wrote that? How do you get it back up?" She clicked the button over and over until it got stuck.

A girl burst out crying. Miss Simpson stopped hammering the remote and looked up. "Who's crying?"

"That's Monica Klatzow," said Terry. "She shouldn't be here today."

"Monica?" said the teacher. "Monica, are you okay?"

"She's not okay," said one of the girls.

"Klatzow was Jessica's dorm-mate," said Wandi. "And her best friend."

Monica cried harder. Miss Simpson passed her the box of tissues from her desk.

"Oh, dear. I need to report this — the message on the board. I need to go up to the office. Candice, please look after the class. I'll be back as soon as I can. Monica, come with me."

They walked up to the admin block together, Monica's cheeks shining with tears, and entered the smart little boardroom where Detective Seko was talking to the headmistress.

"Miss Simpson," said Grashawn, looking up. "You're supposed to be with your class."

"I know. I—"

"Oh, hello, Monica. You poor thing. You really should be at home. Detective? Detective, can we let Monica go home? I believe her parents are waiting for her at the hostel."

"Not until I've interviewed her."

"Mrs Grashawn," says Miss Simpson. "Detective. I need to tell you something. About my classroom."

"What is it?"

"The digital whiteboard. The screen. I rolled it down, and someone had written a message on it. And there was something else, too."

"What did it say?"

"It said—

"It said that it wasn't an accident," said Monica.

Mrs Grashawn went off looking for someone to fix the vandalised screen in Miss Simpson's class while Seko and Simpson sat down with Monica. The detective poured a glass of water for the schoolgirl. "You don't have a very good school record."

Miss Simpson took exception to the comment. "What does that have to do with anything?"

"Smoking. Skipping class. Bunking out. I'm surprised they haven't expelled you."

"I stopped all that," said Monica. "I haven't been in trouble since I started sharing a room with Jess."

"Jessica was the golden girl, huh? Good influence on you?"

"Maybe. She had problems of her own, though."

"Like?"

"She wasn't the golden girl everyone thought she was, okay? That's what you want to hear, isn't it?"

"Tell me why you say that."

"Because you want a reason to blame her for what happened."

"That's not true," said Seko. "All I'm trying to do is get to the bottom of this."

"You're the kind of cop who wants to know what the rape victim was wearing. Because you want to blame the victim."

"Look, Monica," said Miss Simpson. "I know you're overwrought. It's understandable, but—"

"You clearly know something," said Seko. "Why don't you just tell us what it is?"

"It's because of people like you."

The detective didn't break eye contact. "People like me?"

"Bullies!" Monica said, and her eyes filled with tears again.

"What the hell does that mean?"

"Detective, please."

Monica bunched her hands up into fists. "It's because of people like you she committed suicide."

They both stared at the girl, and the tension was broken only when the detective's phone began to ring. He took it outside.

"Listen to me, Monica," said Miss Simpson in a low voice. When the schoolgirl doesn't look at her, she squeezes her arm. "You need to be careful about what you say in here. About speculating. This is a police investigation. You can't just go around spouting assumptions. There may be legal repercussions—"

"I'm not speculating," said Monica. "She told me she was going to do it."

The teacher let go of the girl's arm.

"She told you? Did you tell your parents? Her parents? Mrs Grashawn?"

"She made me swear to keep quiet. She made me blood-promise. She cut my hand here and did the same to herself. And then we mixed blood and promised."

"What did you ... what did she use? To cut?"

"What she always uses. Paul's knife. Paul's pocket knife."

"Who's Paul?"

"Paul's the reason she's dead."

Detective Seko comes back into the room and leans against the wall.

"Tell the detective what you just told me," said the teacher. "Monica. Tell him."

"I need to go to the bathroom," said the girl.

"After you tell him."

"I feel sick. I need to go right now."

Seko took a step forward. "If you would just co-operate, things would—"

Monica doubled over and vomited on the floor.

Miss Simpson shot up, causing her chair to crash backwards. "Oh! You poor thing. I'm sorry. I thought—I didn't know you were really sick."

Detective Seko and Miss Simpson stood in the garden outside the staff room. They watched the water feature in silence as Grashawn approached.

"Nurse Davies said she's fine," said the headmistress. "Nerves, she guesses, and shock. She's keeping her in the sickbay for half an hour till she gets some colour back in her cheeks."

"The poor girl," said Miss Simpson. "Can you imagine?"

"She's hiding something," said Seko.

Grashawn folded her arms. "She's a teenage girl, Detective. Of course she's hiding something." Her phone buzzed with a message; she lowered her glasses to read the screen. "Aha. Paul Compton is here."

Paul Compton was handsome and fresh-faced. Detective Seko smiled at the boy. "Headmistress Grashawn tells me you're in your third year in Chemical Engineering?"

"Yes, sir."

"Top of your class, bright future, all of that?"

"Yes, sir."

"You have everything going for you."

"Do you have a question?" asked the boy. He glanced at his watch. "I ... I have an exam in a couple of hours. It's an important one. I spent so much time preparing, and if I miss it, I'll fail the whole semester and—"

"Yes, I do have a question," said Seko. "If you have all this going for you ... good looks, big brain, wealthy family ... then, tell me, why are you dating a schoolgirl? A girl four years younger than you?"

"Jess and I weren't dating. Not really."

The detective didn't look convinced. "Are you sure about that?"

"I mean, we went out a couple of times."

"And you don't consider that dating?"

"I just mean ... I mean it wasn't official."

"It was pretty official to her," said the cop. "Your name is all over her locker."

"Well," said Paul. "I didn't know that."

"She had your varsity rugby jersey in her dorm."

"Did she?" Paul asked. "I've been looking for that."

Miss Simpson crossed her arms. "She had your pocket knife, too."

Paul swallowed his reply and stared at the floor.

"What exactly was your relationship with Jessica, then?" asked Seko.

"We just ... hung out a few times. Movies. Coffee. That's all."

"It wasn't a sexual relationship?"

"No! No. I mean, I thought she was really pretty but—"

"But?"

"But she was a germ, you know?"

Miss Simpson blinked at him. "A what?"

"A germ. A little kid."

"Jessica Steyn was a beautiful seventeen-year-old girl," said the teacher. "She was not a kid."

"I guess I didn't see her that way. I mean, she's the same age as my little sister."

After dismissing Paul Compton, Detective Seko puts his jacket on. "I'm going to the sickbay. I need to finish the interview with Monica."

"She's ill. Can't you wait till Nurse Davies lets her go?"

"A girl is dead. And I'm going to figure out why. I'm going to see Monica Klatzow. Are you coming?"

They were quiet on the way to the east wing. Nurse Davies looked thrilled to see them and began gushing. "Oh, how exciting! I've never met a real-life detective before. But they're always my favourite shows on the telly. I'm always telling Mr Davies that I'd love to be on the show, you know?"

"Really." Seko managed a polite smile.

"Imagine me as Angela Lansbury, dear, don't you think I would suit the part?"

The nurse hummed the theme music to *Murder She Wrote* as she walked them to Monica's room. The schoolgirl was in the sickbed, skin the colour of the bleached sheets.

"How are you feeling?" asked Miss Simpson. "Better?"

"I've stopped throwing up if that's what you mean."

"We have more questions," said Seko.

"I don't feel up to being interrogated again."

"Believe me," said the cop. "You'd know if this was an interrogation."

Monica looked at the detective and leaned back against the starched cotton pillowcase. "You want to know why someone as pretty and clever and talented as Jess would commit suicide."

"Yes."

"It's not a clear-cut as 'suicide'," said Monica. "There were other ... factors."

"Like?"

"There was someone else."

"What do you mean?" asked Seko. "Who?"

"I feel sick again. I need to go—"

"You're not going anywhere," said Seko. He picked up the steel bin from next to the bed and handed it to the schoolgirl.

"Monica," said Miss Simpson. "When we were speaking earlier, you said *the knife she always uses*. What did you mean? What did Jessica use a pocket knife for?"

"She carried it for protection, but also—"

"For protection?" asked Detective Seko. "From who?"

"I can't tell you."

"You have to tell us."

Monica began to cry. It was a pitiful sound, like a kitten caught in a storm.

The detective lost his patience and stood up. "Pack up your stuff. I'm taking you in."

"Taking her where?" asked Simpson.

"To the station."

"You can't do that! Look at her. She's as pale as—"

"Watch me," said Seko.

"Monica," urged Miss Simpson. "Tell the detective who Jessica needed protection from."

"I can't!" shouted the girl, tears and snot running together. "Don't you understand anything?"

"How can we understand what you're not telling us?!"

"If I tell you, mine will be the next dead body you find."

"Forensics found something—" said Seko. He and Miss Simpson whispered to each other outside the school sick room.

"Yes?"

"It rather complicates the case."

Miss Simpson's phone vibrated with a message, and she was so on edge, she almost dropped it. "I gave my number to the class. Told them to contact me if they wanted to." She squints at the screen. "Hang on. What's this?" She showed the detective the message.

"It's a link to a private video sharing site."

Miss Simpson tapped the icon to play the video. There was murmuring and giggling; skin on sheets.

"What—" said the teacher, wanting to pause it. Seko knocks her hovering hand away.

"Who's it from?" he asked.

"Unknown number." Her jaw dropped. "Is that—?"

They both saw the girl on the video's face at the same time.

"Jessica Steyn," said the detective. She was naked, on a bed. "What's going on?"

A man's voice murmured something indecipherable, and Jessica looked at the camera and laughed. The man joined her, and they kissed.

"So much for thinking of Jessica Steyn as his kid sister," said Seko, speed-dialling the station.

"Who are you phoning?"

"I'm getting my sergeant to drop off Paul Compton at the station."

~

"Monica," said Miss Simpson. "Why didn't you tell us about the video?"

"Which vid—?"

"Don't play dumb," barks Seko. "Do you want us to find who did this to Jessica or not?"

Miss Simpson blinked at the girl. "The video's on the internet, now, you know. Once something is on the internet, you can never take it off. Who posted it? Did Paul post it?"

"No!" insisted Monica. "He would never. He loved Jess."

Seko spoke slowly and deliberately. "Who — posted — the — video?"

"I don't know," said Monica. "I promise you I don't know. But—"

"Paul's at the police station. He lied to us about his relationship with Jessica and now he's being interviewed by someone a lot bigger and nastier than I am. Would you like to end up there, too? Spend the night in a cold prison cell? Sleep on the stained concrete floor?"

"Please, no. I just want to go home."

"Tell us what you know, and we'll let you go. It's as simple as that."

"You won't believe me!" Her hands flew up to her hair, and Simpson noticed her nails were bitten right down. She took the schoolgirl by the shoulders. "Monica. Pull yourself together. Tell us what you know."

There was a long pause, then Monica whispered. "The Hollow Man."

"What?"

"The Hollow Man killed her."

The hairs on the back of Miss Simpson's neck stood up. "Who's ... the Hollow Man?"

"A figment of imagination," said Seko. "The school grounds are secure. No one from the outside can get in, and there was no sign of any security breach."

"The Hollow Man doesn't need to break in."

The detective frowned in irritation. "What?"

"He's here all the time. He comes out at night. He catches us in our dreams."

Detective Seko and Miss Simpson marched over to the headmistress's office and stuck their heads in, interrupting her on the phone. "Ah, hello, Detective. Miss Simpson. Are you getting anywhere? How much longer till I can release my pupils?

"We're getting somewhere," said the cop.

"Good, because my phone is ringing off the hook with anxious parents and press and goodness knows who else. Have you seen them? There's a whole crowd gathered outside."

"They can wait," said Seko.

Mrs Grashawn's mobile phone rang again, and she muted it. "Wait? Easy for you to say! How would you feel if your daughter was locked up in a school where a girl was found dead?"

"I'd be happy that the police were investigating her murder," replied Seko.

"What?" said the headmistress, clutching her desk. "What did you just say?"

"According to Monica Klatzow, there's been a man coming into the dormitories at night."

"Impossible!" said Grashawn, wilting with shock.

"There's no evidence whatsoever of any outside element," said Seko, adjusting his tie. "I need to speak to her classmates."

"Angela," said Seko. "I think it would be best if we split forces."

Miss Simpson stopped. "You don't want me in the interview with the three girls?"

"It's not that," said the cop. "I just think that you're the one who needs to speak to Monica again."

"But she's not saying a word. She's practically catatonic. I don't even know if Nurse Davies will let me back in there. What makes you think—"

"She's clearly got an issue with authority figures." He tapped his police badge. "This isn't helping."

"All right," said Miss Simpson. "I'll try."

"Before you go—"

She turned back to Seko. "Yes?"

"Earlier, when you were talking about the whiteboard in your class. That someone wrote on."

"Yes?"

"We were interrupted. You were about to say that there was something else."

"Oh, yes. There was also a strange sign drawn next to the words. A circle with some lines through it. Like an 'H' and—"

Seko showed her his phone screen. "Like this?"

"That's it," said Miss Simpson. "How do you have it on your phone? Where was that taken?"

"You don't want to know."

"Try me."

"The forensic team found it carved into Jessica's back."

Her hand flew up to her mouth. "No."

"I didn't know what it was until Monica told us about the Hollow Man."

"What?"

"Can't you see? Inside the circle, those lines: it's an 'H' and an 'M'. Hollow Man."

Seko eyed the schoolgirls one by one. "So, girls," he said. "Tell me about the Hollow Man."

"He's not real," said Candice, the head girl.

"What are you talking about?" said Wandi. "Of course he's real! Who else would have—"

Seko looked at her. "Yes?"

"The Hollow Man was cutting her," said Wandi, fear dancing in her dark eyes.

Terry nodded. "That's what she said. The Hollow Man was hurting her at night."

"You guys are insane," said Candice.

"He'd cut her in secret places that no one could see," said Monica. "These fine cuts. Her scalp. The soles of her feet. In between her fingers."

"Ask Monica," said Terry. "She knows."

"I know you're feeling vulnerable," said Miss Simpson. "I want you to know that I'll keep you safe."

"You can't keep me safe," said Monica. "No one can."

Miss Simpson adjusts her position in her seat. "Tell me more about the Hollow Man."

"Why? It's not like anyone believes me."

"Is it someone you know? How does he get in? How long had he been hurting Jessica?"

Monica shook her head. "I don't know him. He's like ... he's like a ghost, like cold black smoke, that comes in through the window."

"You've seen him?"

"No. I've felt him, though. It's like when he's in the room your blood just runs cold."

"Has he ever hurt you?"

"No. No. He wanted Jess. But he'll come for me now that she's gone."

"You'll be home, safe," said Miss Simpson.

"He doesn't care. It doesn't matter where you are. He got Jess at the swimming hall. He can get you anywhere."

"Have any of you ever seen the Hollow Man?" asked detective Seko.

Wandi replied. "You can't see him, except in your dreams."

"He's like a ghost," said Terry.

"So, you've never seen him," said Seko. "Never had any evidence of him."

"Sometimes we can feel him around us," said Wandi. "Like, you know that feeling? When there is evil around you. You can just feel it."

Seko shifted in his seat. "Tell me about the video."

"Jessica was really upset about the video," said Terry. "She was worried that her parents would see it. Or that it would come up in the Olympic team selection, or future job interviews."

Wandi rubbed her forehead. "It made her sick."

Detective Seko banged a book on the table, making them all jump in their seats.

"What's that?" asked Terry.

"It's a diary."

Wandi looked nervous. "Jessica's diary?"

"That's right. One of my men found it under Jessica's mattress. I haven't had time to read the whole thing yet." He paged through the handwritten pages slowly for effect. "Now, why are you girls suddenly looking nervous?"

Nurse Davies entered the sick-room balancing two steaming mugs of tea, then tapped the face of her watch at Miss Simpson. Her meaning was clear: *leave the poor girl alone.* Once she had left and closed the door behind her, Miss Simpson leaned forward.

"Monica. I know this is difficult to talk about, but I need you to tell me about the bullying."

The girl swallowed hard. "What bullying?"

"We've read some of Jessica's diary. We know how bad it was getting. You can tell me anything."

~

"You know what?" asked Seko.

"What?" asked Candice, arms still crossed.

"Jessica wrote in her journal "they" wouldn't leave her alone. "The Mean Girls" she called them. Any idea who these three mean girls could be?"

"No," said Wandi.

"You know, she actually saved us the trouble of guessing. Look here. These three dark scribbles, like shadows ... what did you call it? Like cold black smoke. But these have names. Look. Terry, Wandile, Candice."

"I don't know why she would have drawn that."

"You don't know? Really? Here, I'll give you a clue." He picked up the diary and began to read from it. *"They're making life so difficult for me. I don't know why. I don't know what I've done to them.* And here's another one: *Today Terry emptied my dustbin on my bed. Said that I was a dirty slut, and that I deserved to sleep in filth."*

Terry chewed her lip. "Um, that didn't happen—"

"Wandi and Terry stripped my locker today. They just threw all my stuff on the floor, including my panties from gym the day before. My box of tampons. I don't know how many people saw the mess before I found it. I'm so embarrassed."

"Well," said Wandi. "We had to teach her a lesson."

"Shut up, Wandi!" shouted Candice.

"Teach her a lesson?" asked Seko. "Why?"

"Because she was—"

"If you don't shut up right now, Wandi, I'll—"

"When I got into bed last night, there was a dead mouse under the duvet. I only realised when my leg was touching it, and then I jumped out and screamed. There was blood on the sheets. The Mean Girls didn't even hide the fact that they were laughing."

"That was just a practical joke," said Terry.

"That doesn't sound like a joke to me."

"She was sleeping around," murmured Wandi.

Terry turned to Seko. "With all due respect, Detective. Wolverhampton has the best reputation in the country; we must keep it that way. She was meeting Paul in the school swimming hall! Having sex on the premises! We warned her to stop, but she didn't listen."

"That video was the last straw," said Wandi. "When people put two and two together they will realise that Jess was a Wolverhampton girl and that's it, down goes the reputation of the school and everyone in it."

Seko picked up the diary again. *"They took my towel and my clothes when I was showering today. I had to walk all the way down the corridor naked, my scars on show. Just before I reached my dorm, they started throwing the clothes at me like rotten tomatoes. Calling me a whore. I can't live like this anymore."*

"It's not like we didn't give her a choice," sneered Candice. "All she had to do was stop being a dirty little slut."

"Ah," Seko released a satisfied sigh. "Finally. I see the real Candice Compton. I've been waiting for you to drop your act."

"Well, good for you."

"You have a lot of people fooled, with your head girl's badge and blazer full of scrolls."

"Are you finished?" she demanded. "Can we go now?"

Seko stretched his arms above his head. "Yes."

"Yes?" said Terry. "Really?"

"Well, it's not like he can keep us indefinitely," said Candice. "My parents would have him out of a job in seconds."

"Are your parents bullies, like you are?" asked Seko.

Candice pursed her lips and stood up to leave. "You'll find out, soon enough."

"Wait," said Miss Simpson. "Sit down. We have a deal for you."

"That key to the swimming pool gate," said Seko. "It never turned up, did it?"

Simpson shook her head. "No."

"So there *was* someone with her there, this morning. And that person took the key."

Miss Simpson looked into his eyes. "And ghosts can't take keys, can they?"

Monica sat with her feet in the cold pool water, thinking of Jessica. The three mean girls arrived, swaggering and sneering. Monica jolted when she saw them.

"Why so on edge?" asked Terry.

"Wouldn't you be?" Monica replied. "After what happened?"

"Nope. Not on edge. Not even nervous," said Candice. "You know why?"

"Why?"

"Because I'm not scared of ghosts."

"Well," said Monica, her eyes darting around. "Well, you should be." She swung her legs out of the pool and stood up to face them.

Candice laughed. "You think you got away with it, don't you?"

"Got away with what?" asked Monica, wide-eyed.

"Don't play dumb, Monica," said Wandi. "You know exactly what we're talking about."

"What are you guys even doing here?"

"What are *you* doing here, Klatzow?" asked Candice. "Checking out the scene of the crime? Shouldn't you be at home?"

Wandi nodded. "Especially in your ... *condition.*"

The other girls sniggered.

"What ... what are you talking about?" asked Monica, looking ill again.

Wandi approached her, touching the front of her school uniform. "You think you can hide it under that baggy school jersey?"

Monica pushed Wandi's hand away. "Leave me alone!"

"Unless you're just putting on weight," said Terry. "I've seen how much tuck you've been eating. Are you getting fat? Is that why you don't shower at the hostel anymore?"

The mean girls snigger again.

"You think you can hide your stink?" asked Candice. "Well, you can't. We can smell your vomit from a mile away."

"Shut up," shouted Monica. "All of you. Just shut up!"

"Do you even know who the father is?"

"Of course I know who the father is!"

"So, you admit it," said Candice. "You're pregnant."

Monica glared at them, her hands shaking.

"I knew it," said Wandi. "You're a scabby slut, just like Jessica was."

Monica slapped Wandi through the face, shocking them both.

"You little bitch!" whispered Wandi.

"Come near me, and I'll hit you again. Any of you!"

"Is it true?" asked Paul, who no one had noticed arrive.

"Paul!" Candice says to her brother. "What the hell are *you* doing here?"

Paul pushed past his sister and stood in front of Monica. "Is it true, Monica? You're ... pregnant? Were you ever going to tell me?"

"I was going to tell you. When you asked me to meet you here, I thought it would be the perfect time. I didn't tell you before because—"

Candice guffawed. "You can't be serious." When he didn't reply, her smile faded. "Paul? It's your baby?"

Terry laughed. It was an ugly sound. Candice whipped around to confront her. "What are you laughing at?"

"Well, it's kind of funny, don't you think? I mean, you're going to be an aunt. You'll be family with this—"

"Over my dead body!"

Monica narrowed her eyes at Candice. "I hope the Hollow Man heard you say that."

"Shut up about your stupid Hollow Man. Your stupid game. It's over. No one believed you, anyway."

"Jessica believed me," said Monica.

"You know, I never understood that," said Candice.

"What?"

"Why you tormented Jessica. I mean, wasn't she supposed to be your best friend?"

"She was my best friend. Yes."

"So why did you do all those terrible things to her?"

"I wasn't the one bullying her and making her life impossible. She killed herself because of what you three did to her. She told me she couldn't handle it anymore. And then just as she was at breaking point, you posted that video of her and Paul."

"She deserved that," said Terry.

"I knew immediately that it was you who did it, Candice. I mean who else could have copied that clip from Paul's phone?"

Paul ground his teeth and clenched his fists. "You did that? How could you?"

"Jess told me she couldn't live with the bullying anymore," said Monica. "The one thing that was keeping her going was her Olympic team selection. She couldn't wait to go to that training camp. But then you posted that video, and she knew it was just a matter of time before they found out and cancelled her contract. No way they'd let that kind of scandal mar their reputation. Getting on that team was her last hope of getting away from you, and you took that away from her. That's why she killed herself."

Candice pursed her lips and did a slow clap. "Bravo, bravo. What a speech. Well done. But I think we all know that's not true."

"Jessica was murdered," said Paul. "That's what the cops at the station told me. They have evidence that she was knocked out and drowned."

"Monica knows full well that it wasn't suicide," said Candice. "Don't you, you little freak?"

Monica clenched her jaw. "Don't call me that."

"Truth hurts?"

"Leave her alone," said Paul. "She's been through enough. Come on. It's time to go home."

"I don't think she's been through nearly enough," said Candice. "It's funny, you know, Paul. Mom and Dad think you're so damn smart ... but when it comes to girls, you're so naïve."

Paul frowned at his sister. "What do you mean?"

"This freak has been playing you like Candy Crush."

Terry nodded. "She's been playing everybody."

"How did she get you to sleep with her? Let me guess. She showed up here in the swimming hall one evening when you were supposed to be meeting Jess, and she was crying about something, right?"

Paul didn't answer.

"And you took pity on her and hugged her, and one thing led to the next and what do you know? ... Bam! She's pregnant. Now she's got all the ammo she needs to blackmail you into a relationship with her."

"That's not what it's about," said Monica.

"She's a freak from a freak family, Paul. And they have no money. Then she met you. A handsome boy with a bright future, and family with more money than she's ever comprehended. And suddenly she stops smoking at school and she starts wearing nice clothes—"

"—Jessica's clothes—" added Wandi.

"And hanging out at the swimming hall when she doesn't even know how to swim. Open your eyes, Paul!"

Pauls runs his fingers through his floppy hair. "I—"

"But there was a problem, wasn't there, Monica? An obstacle. Someone was standing in your way, and you had to get rid of her."

Paul laughed. "You're not serious. You can't believe that—"

"So you started tormenting Jessica," said Candice.

"I wasn't the one bullying her. You were!"

"Right," said Candice. "You were the one scaring her. The one driving her crazy with your stupid Hollow Man story so you could have Paul all to yourself."

Monica shook her head. "You're the one who's crazy."

"You can deny it all you like," said Candice. "At first, when I heard the Hollow Man story, I thought, wow! That's original. You're creative. Maybe you do have some kind of redeeming quality. But then I Googled 'Hollow Man' and saw that you didn't think him up yourself. You just found a scary story on the internet and put a twist on it."

"You can't prove anything," said Monica.

"You're right. But that doesn't mean you won't be locked up for a long, long time."

"I can't go to prison," said Monica. "I'm pregnant."

"Was she ever really your best friend? I think she just felt sorry for you, and you took full advantage."

"I won't have this baby in prison."

There was a scuffle and a glinting blade in Monica's hand.

"Watch out!" yelled Terry.

"Hey," said Paul. "That's my pocket knife. Where did you get it?"

"Where do you think she got it? She stole it from Jessica just like she did everything else."

The girls advanced on Monica, and she held the knife up in her shaking hand.

Detective Seko crept out from behind the wall, gun aimed at Monica. "Put the knife down, Klatzow."

"Listen to what the detective says, Monica," says Simpson, who is a few steps behind him. "I've recorded everything on my phone. Put it down before anyone gets hurt."

"They deserve to get hurt!" shouted Monica. "Years and years of bullying. They made me into what I am."

"Put the knife down," said Miss Simpson, pulling a pair of handcuffs from her jacket pocket. A badge flashed from inside the garment.

"I can't. I can't go to prison." Monica wrestled with herself, and Paul's pocketknife fell from her hand and clattered on the poolside tiles. Simpson picked it up and sealed it in an evidence bag.

Monica stared at Paul, her pain at being betrayed twisting her face into a grimace. "You set me up?"

"The cops made me call you. Made me agree to meet you here. They'd have pressed charges, otherwise. About the video. I can't have a criminal record!"

"I got the same deal," said Candice. "Get a confession out of you, and I'll skip jail time."

"You bastards," Monica said.

"Oh, please," said Candice. "Don't play the victim. You killed Jessica. You deserve to go to prison."

"Good work, partner," said Seko. Simpson nodded. She liked being undercover; enjoyed acting different parts — mechanic, shopkeeper, accountant, temp teacher.

"Come on," Simpson said, cuffing Monica's hands behind her back. "Let's go."

Monica struggled against her. "I can't go to jail. I can't be alone!"

"Don't worry," said Candice. "I'm sure the Hollow Man will keep you company."

6

THE WHITE MOUSE

Akeratu

Silok, 2051

Jana stood outside, surveying what remained of her garden. She picked a leaf from the gnarled plum tree and examined it. The perforated paper flag was scorched by the acidic ash that snowed endlessly down from the toxic fog above. The veins of the leaf were still intact, creating the illusion of a delicate skeleton made of only dried brown costa; a transparent butterfly's wing. The rain would eat pretty patterns into anything it touched. Gazing at the garden sometimes felt like a sinister version of hunting for pictures in the clouds.

Jana knew there was a certain beauty in destruction, but not in this. She released it, and the leaf fluttered down to the yellow grass while she dusted her fingers of its residue. The apple trees were the first to go, then the fig. The plum had held out for the longest but was now also succumbing to the sour air that swirled around it. Jana needed no further reminders of death.

She closed her eyes to remember the taste of the syrupy purple plums, and how the yard used to look: a lush jungle with not a brick nor patch of plaster showing—as if someone had painted it a verdant green. It was not uncommon in the 2030s to have a forest in one's backyard. The community of Silok had taken up their spades in response to the mayor's plea to plant carbon-trapping food gardens. The suburb had exploded with shoots and leaves and vigorous climbers. The community swapped slips and saplings and eventually bartered produce: carrots; coriander; compost. Rosy apples and jade plants. It had brought them together in a way technology never had, but the invading silver soldiers had subverted that. The State of Shengdu had pitted neighbours against one other, and those neighbours fed whispers to the enemy in the empty hope their families would be safe. Now they passed on suspicion instead of seeds.

Jana had never expected to be a wife—and certainly never a mother— but life had a way of surprising her with gifts as much as it did by taking them away. She never guessed she'd have two small children. Few people knew that before the occupation of western Akeratu, Jana had been an SOE for the resistance movement. In a seemingly different lifetime, they nicknamed her *The White Mouse* because of her ability to evade capture. The meek moniker had been at odds with her personality. At that time, Jana had been a hard-drinking, foul- mouthed blonde bombshell. But the nickname resonated on a deep level because no matter how hard she tried to forget it, she remem- bered growing up with the mousy girl in the mirror; the raggedy-ann dresses, the limp plaits and hunger pangs. In the quieter moments of her life as a high-society hostess and Special Operations Executive, her nickname reminded her how far she had come, and for what she was fighting.

Jana saved fellow resistance fighters and downed airmen. She passed on classified information gleaned from late-night drinks with Sheng officials to the rebel intelligence. Once, she'd ordered the execution of a female spy working to undermine their resistance, and it hadn't even put her off her breakfast. It was a different time, bold and exploding with the sparks of danger, and maybe that's why she had fallen so hard for Kino when he was introduced to her by a fellow rebel.

It wasn't Kino's dark, handsome face that made her heart beat faster. He had a way about him: tender, funny, authentic, and an excellent shot with the customised pistol he'd taken off a silver soldier in an unsuccessful raid. Kino refused to file off the silver swastika that decorated its handle; said it brought him luck. Jana told him it attracted trouble.

Kino had grinned. *It's the same thing, isn't it?*

It was the unborn baby who saved the rebels' lives. As Kitsune grew in Jana's womb, Kino was moved to propose by candlelight. He painted a picture of how they could remove themselves from the relentlessness of the rebellion. Jana held the belief she would die progressing the resistance movement; couldn't see a different ending to the mission she had accepted when the Sheng State began sending its toxic tendrils into her homeland. But Kino described an alternative vision; one free of constant peril, and she took the ticket he offered her. They would make an attempt at an ordinary life—or as ordinary as the State allowed—and spend a few years loving each other and the child before the inevitable happened.

Their comrades were not bitter. Perhaps they were too exhausted for wasteful emotions, or maybe it gave them hope that one day they could also return to a normal life. Soon Jana and Kino were married and living together in a small house with a young blossoming plum tree in the backyard.

As the blossoms turned to fruit, Jana's taut body softened and swelled. When Kitsune was born after a long, dark labour, Jana and Kino wept in each other's arms. Crashing rapids of hope and despair overcame them. As they cradled the sleeping baby, their eyes said the same thing: *What have we done?*

The future was bleaker than it had ever been, with silver soldiers banging their rifle butts on the neighbour's doors at midnight. It was a terrible, terrifying sound. The chorus of catastrophe would haunt Jana's dreams. They heard snatches of stories of how soldiers dragged families from their beds to be separated, or shot. Any hint of suspicion was enough to warrant being "collected" by the State. Jana and Kino knew it was just a matter of time before the invaders came for them. The plan had been to leave the resistance movement, but after Kitsune was born, and then his little sister Milla, Jana and Kino realised they had more than ever to fight for. Kino never spoke about his operations, he never had. His biggest fear was Jana being tortured for information. Jana could no longer be the glamorous hostess she had played before, but she still had contacts. She drafted pamphlets which would then be copied and distributed to fellow rebels. If anyone asked, she called herself a freelance journalist.

The stories were an essential part of fighting the indoctrination of the Shengdu propaganda. The State would have you believe that everyone East of the Fiume river was living in a State-sponsored Shangri-La. Of course, this was not true. The people there had access to medical care, clean water, and fresh food, but it came at a cost. The citizens' thoughts were censored; their bodies policed.

On the day Jana was writing up a new story about a schoolgirl who had been raped and impregnated by a fellow student, and she felt the danger humming in her veins. In the Silver State, abortion was punishable by death, and the rapist had been granted visitation rights, including being allowed to attend the birth. Jana's jaw ached, and she realised she was clenching it as she typed. She imagined herself in that situation, and then her daughter, and bitterness climbed up her throat. There had been a slew of shameful stories leaking that month, including smuggled pictures of dull-eyed children kept in cages. Jana stopped writing and stood up. Her idea was to get some fresh air outside, in the garden, but the state of the plum tree just highlighted her despair. Specks of grey floated down from the sky. What kind of life were they living?

"Mama?" came a voice from behind Jana, and she spun around.

"Don't come out," said Jana, walking up to the toddler and lifting her small body into a hug. She thinks of the brown leaf shot through with holes. "Don't go outside, okay?"

When did the weather become something to be feared? As if there wasn't enough to worry about.

With the last of the flour ration, they baked some bread together, and when Kitsune ambled in, hands in pockets, he smiled hopefully at the aroma. Jana took the loaf out of the oven, and as they waited for it to cool, the doorbell rang. Jana cautiously opened to three smudge-cheeked children. "Food," they muttered. There was no room in their desperation for *please.*

Jana told them to wait, then cut the loaf in half and bundled it up in a faded tea towel.

Kitsune blocked her way. "You can't give that to them," he said. "The cupboards are bare. We won't get more rations till Friday."

A gaping hole of three days stretched before them. Jana forced words past the lump in her throat. "They're starving."

"So are we!" said Kitsune, tears in his eyes. "What about your teeth? And you said yourself that Milla isn't growing."

Jana bit her lip to hide her shock. What else had he overheard? She lowered herself, balancing on a knee, and pulled his face towards hers so that their foreheads were touching; her arm wrapped around his small frame. "They're starving, Kitsune," she repeated. "Their parents are dead."

Mouth down-turned, he blinked forcefully, trying to get rid of the tears. "Yes, Mama," he said and moved out of her way. Her tongue moved involuntarily to her loose molar, testing its attachment. It would be the third tooth she lost to poor nutrition and pollution. The doorstep children grabbed the chunk of the warm loaf and ran away. They did not say thank you. When Kino arrived home, his face a thunderbolt, the kitchen still smelt like freshly baked bread.

"What is it?" asked Jana, wiping her hands after putting the children to bed, trying to put out of her mind the smallness of Milla's body under the faded blue blanket. Kino just stared out the kitchen window. She moved towards him and touched his back, and he startled.

His expression chilled her. "Kino?"

Her husband looked at her, then rubbed his face. "I got the note today."

"No," she said. Jana's insides were ice water.

Kino nodded.

I got the note today.

The phrase was their emergency flare, fizzing between them, asserting its ugly truth. Their family were to be collected that night—or perhaps the next—but they had finally made the list everyone in Silok feared. They had discussed this day, planned every detail, but still, it didn't feel real. Their emergency bags were packed and hidden in the crawl-space under the wooden floor. Jana's stomach roiled.

"It was one of the pamphlets you wrote," he said. "It got into the wrong hands." There was nothing accusatory in his tone. They were rebels when they fell in love, and they always knew they would die for what they believed. The children, however, made it almost impossible to bear.

A part of her, the hopeless part, made her want to give up. She didn't want to put her children through the terror of running for their lives. Some parents had taken a hot iron to the back of their children's necks to burn the barcodes off, hoping it would save them. It hadn't.

"We will not panic," said Jana, more to herself than anyone else. "We know what to do."

"Yes," said Kino. His eyes were soft; his touch tender. That happens when you know you only have one more night with the love of your life. He fetched an old bottle of plum brandy from the kitchen. Alcohol hadn't been available to buy since the Sheng shut down the industry, but Jana and Kino had distilled some from the fruit of their tree before it stopped producing. They had been saving it for the day the war ended; a victory drink. He wiped the oily dust from the bottle and set out two scuffed glass tumblers on the kitchen counter, pouring them a syrupy shot each. They settled in the living room, looking out into the skeletal branches of the dead garden, sipping the brandy while Kino massaged Jana's feet. They had revised the plan hundreds of times and were never satisfied. There didn't seem to be a plan that wasn't cruel.

"You leave at midnight," said Jana. "You take Milla with you." Tears rushed, but she blinked them away. "I leave in the morning with Kitsune."

If the silver soldiers found all four of them on the streets, they'd realise they were running, scan their barcodes, and put them in detention. It's why they had to split up. The plan was to reunite somewhere on the other side of danger, but unfortunately, they didn't know where that was.

"What if we never see each other again?" asked Jana.

"Then at least we've given our kids a chance to survive."

"What kind of life is that to live? On the run, scared, not knowing where you'll sleep or if you'll eat?" She imagined Milla being hungry, and it broke her heart. Her frame was already so tiny. "What's the point?"

"They'll be alive," said Kino. "That's the point."

"Maybe being alive is overrated," said Jana.

"You don't believe that."

"I do," said Jana. "I don't want the kids to suffer."

He sighed. "Nor do I."

"So why not end our terror, and theirs?"

Kino stopped rubbing her feet. "What are you saying?"

"You know what I'm saying. We have cyanide."

"No," Kino said, shaking his head.

"We can end the terror tonight. Wake them up, eat whatever is left in the house. A farewell feast and a special drink. Then we can all cuddle up together and fall asleep and never again have to worry about tomorrow—"

Kino pulled his wife towards him and crushed her in a hug. She stopped talking. They wept into each other's arms, touching their faces together, their palms, their chests. Kino's stubble scraped Jana's cheek, and she cried from the familiar comfort of it; the scent of his warm skin. He inhaled her hair. Impossible to believe it would be the last time they were together, they made love slowly, carefully, exalting each other's bodies; the skin they knew so well. It was not about pleasure—although there was that, too—it was instead the most intimate of goodbyes.

Afterwards, they poured one last drink. There was little point in trying to sleep. They sat folded into one another and spoke softly. Jana's loose tooth niggled her as her tongue found it over and over again.

"Your tooth bothering you?" asked Kino.

Jana nodded. "I should just pull the thing out."

It had horrified her when she lost a tooth a year ago. Every time her tongue touched the residual bloody gum recess, she got a little shock. There were no longer dentists in Silok; not that it would have helped. The doctor would have prescribed fresh fruit and vegetables, or supplements, but those were not available either. Eventually, Jana had to resign herself to the fact that she would slowly lose her teeth just as the plum tree dropped the last of its acidic globes. It was the price you paid for not being born on the "right" side of the river; of not betraying your people by defecting and joining the Sheng.

Some former neighbours had done that; had been brainwashed by the Sheng to believe that life was better in eastern Akeratu, where your every move was recorded, measured, evaluated—social engineering masquerading as public health. Where you'd thank the State for their provisions, forever dependent on their daily rations of food and water. Jana couldn't imagine living like that. She grimaced at the feeling of her errant tooth.

Kino stroked Jana's hair. "Would you like me to pull it out for you?"

She shook her head. It would be a relief to get rid of it, but her memory of their last night together was more important to her. Jana pulled her hair back with an old rubber elastic band and wiped her face. Kino's eyes bored into her, making her feel self-conscious.

"I'm a mess," she said.

"Nonsense," uttered Kino, catching her hand. "You've never been more beautiful. Rebellion has made the best of you, and motherhood has made you bloom. I've never admired you more."

When Kino was ready to leave, Jana wrapped Milla Mouse in a blanket and tied her to Kino's back. She draped a thin rubber rain jacket around his shoulders.

"Go well," she said. There were no tears in her eyes, but she could feel herself breaking. Watching Kino leave with apple-cheeked Milla was the very worst moment of her life. Her heart ached so hard she clutched her chest and wondered if she was having a heart attack. Jana sunk to her knees and then collapsed on the floor, cheek-to-floorboard. Only then the tears came.

"Mama?" asked Kitsune. "Mama?"

Jana started, her body stiff from hours of lying on the hard floor. She opened her stinging eyes. The sun was rising. "What time is it?" she asked. "We've got to go. We've got to go."

"Milla's not in her bed," said Kitsune. "I can't find her."

Jana swallowed hard, took his soft hands in hers. "They've already left. We'll meet up with them."

"What?" he asked. "Where?"

Jana removed her necklace with the locket from around her neck and clipped it around Kitsune's. "We're going on an adventure, just you and I."

They were about to leave when they heard it. The deafening noise of the silver soldiers smashing the butts of their rifles on the door, ready to break right through the timber. Jana grabbed Kitsune's small shoulders and whispered: "Go hide in the kennel!"

The boy tried to argue, but she hissed at him and shoved Kitsune in the direction of the courtyard. She watched as her son scurried away, then turned to face the silver soldiers who had just splintered the door. She began shouting at them, and they returned her words with bullets. Milla and Kitsune were on her mind; Kino's scent was still on her cheeks and lips. After the bullets hit, Jana expected relief, but there was just pain as her chest exploded like a blooming flower, arching and opening its blood red petals. With a final shout and a raised fist against the Silver State, Jana fell, and her soul splashed out of her body.

7

THE PATRON SAINT OF CHILDREN

FATHER SANDERSON's foot vibrated silently against the floor. He ran his index finger between his neck and priest's collar, which felt too tight against his skin. The air was stale and scented as always by incense holders, balding velvet, books and candle wax. If only he could stop his heart from beating so fast. The bishop glared at him from the visitor's chair across his mahogany desk, the warm light above them highlighting the silver in his hair and his unswerving nose. Father Sanderson hoped that bishop Francis could not smell the sweat that stained the shirt he was wearing beneath his cassock. No longer able to sit still, the priest rose and made his way to a nondescript cupboard near the filing cabinet. A small key unlocked the door and travelled back to the priest's pocket. He brought out two small glasses and a bottle of dry sherry, which he offered to the bishop without speaking. Bishop Francis was able to nod and look disapproving at the same time.

The priest turned his back on the old man so he wouldn't notice if his fingers shook while pouring. He would have poured himself a drink before the impromptu meeting, to steady his nerves, but he knew he'd be driving that night, so he had reluctantly abstained. When he sat down, a sigh escaped the priest's lips.

"I assume you know why I asked to see you," said the bishop, his long wiry eyebrows knitting in an accusing way. His raptorial eyes were unblinking.

"Yes, Your Excellency," Father Sanderson said. "It is unfortunate."

"Unfortunate, indeed," said Bishop Francis. "This report could be a significant problem for Stuart Hall."

"Yes," agreed the priest and took a shaky sip of his sherry. Despite the clear crimson liquid on his tongue, his mouth remained dry.

"I'm going to have to ask you a few questions."

"Of course," said Father Sanderson. Suddenly impatient with his trembling hands, he threw the rest of his sherry down his throat and was glad to be rid of the glass. His foot was still vibrating.

"As you know, Sister Agnes had a complaint from one of the boys."

The priest and the bishop locked eyes.

"Inappropriate conduct," the grey-haired man continued, his mouth a hard line, "in the vestry."

"I was informed," said Father Sanderson. "But apparently the boy— Ethan—would not say who perpetrated the act."

Perspiration continued to spread beneath his cassock, and he could now smell the sourness emanating from his body.

"Father Sanderson," said the bishop. "I can see you are going through a dark night of the soul. I have to ask you. Was it you who interfered with the boy?"

"No," said the priest, without hesitation. "It was not me, Your Excellency. It will never be me. I have within me neither the desire nor the brutality to do such a thing."

The bishop seemed satisfied with that, although he had not yet leaned back in the chair or touched his sherry. "Of course, it's possible that the boy is being dishonest."

"Yes," said Father Sanderson.

"Jesus loves hidden souls," said the bishop. "A hidden flower is the most fragrant."

Sanderson wondered where his car keys were, and how much fuel he had in the tank. The bishop was waiting for a response from him. Eventually, he said: "The boys at Stuart Hall are not always honest."

Bishop Francis finally relaxed in his chair with a slump. "Not even his own parents believe his story. They say he deserves a good beating for making up such terrible things."

"Beating? He's seven years old."

"Ethan's had his share of troubles. He's not the most trustworthy boy in the school, is he?"

"I suppose not," said Sanderson.

"They said he shouldn't be allowed to go home this weekend."

"The parents said that?"

"Yes. It was no shock to Ethan. I'll spend some time with the boy tomorrow. See what I can do to stop this from happening again."

Sanderson nodded. "Good idea."

"I think we have this figured out, then."

"All right," said Sanderson, relieved. "*Deo gratias.*"

"*Deo gratias.*" Bishop Francis swigged his sherry and stood up to leave. "I'll see you at mass. I pray that God may preserve your health and life for many years. All our blessings come to us through our Lord."

Sanderson walked around the table. "Thank you, Your Excellency."

When the bishop left, it felt like the whole room exhaled. Father Sanderson checked the corridor to be certain he was gone, then turned back to face the room.

The boy's pale face surfaced from beneath the gold tassels that hung from the tablecloth covering the front of the desk.

"Ethan," said Father Sanderson. "Come."

They hurried down the corridor which had just moments before hosted the bishop's footfall. The priest bundled the boy into his car, an old Toyota with paint chips and a small crack in the windscreen. He lobbed a black satchel onto the back seat, then clicked the boy's safety belt in, made him lie down, and covered him with a blanket. The car started on the second try, and the priest did not switch on the headlights. They drove slowly out of the Stuart Hall grounds. When he was sure no one had noticed their departure, Father Sanderson rolled down his window. He took in huge gulps of fresh air, so fresh-tasting compared to that in his claustrophobic study.

Two hours later, they reached the motel the priest had booked ahead of time. He always used the same motel; this was his seventh visit. He woke Ethan, and they went inside the dingy room. They both sat on the ends of their single beds, facing each other. The priest's foot was tapping the floor again.

"You ready?" asked Father Sanderson.

"Yes," said the boy and began to take off his clothes.

"Wait," said the priest. "We'll do your hair first."

The priest opened his satchel and took out a pair of scissors and a box of black hair dye. He coloured the boy's hair, washed it, then cut it short. It wasn't the best haircut in the world, but it would do. When Ethan stripped, the priest threw his clothes in the bin and gave him the new outfit he had bought. They snapped off the price tags together. Once the boy had dressed, Father Sanderson boiled water and made them both some of the motel's cheap hot chocolate while they waited. It tasted thin and too sweet, but it was a comfort all the same.

Finally, there was a knock on the door. A woman's soft voice said, "Saint Nicholas."

Ethan looked up at the priest, and he nodded. The password they had agreed on was correct: the patron saint of children.

Father Sanderson opened the door and handed the boy over to the woman who stood there.

"This is Sister Lindsay," said the priest.

She was smiling as she took hold of Ethan's thin shoulders. "It's just Lindsay. I'm not a nun anymore."

The boy looked up at Father Sanderson, an indecipherable expression on his face.

"Go well, Ethan," said the priest. "May the Lord protect you." He put his hand on the boy's head as if it were a last benediction. "You'll never have to see Bishop Francis again."

Ethan began to sob; his whole body seemed to sag in relief. The woman's eyes shone with tears as the priest handed her the small black rucksack and looked at his watch. "I need to get back before they notice I'm gone."

"Of course," said the social worker. "Travel safely."

It was a difficult thing to do in life: travel safely. Especially when the people who were supposed to be protecting you were the ones inflicting the wounds.

"Thank you," he said.

"It's a good thing you're doing, Father," she said, and bundled Ethan into her car.

It's a good thing. He wanted to find some kind of satisfaction in this. Still, as he thought of Bishop Francis's predatory eyes, he knew it was not enough.

8

SCHRÖDINGER DREAM

THIS STORY IS AN ADAPTED *excerpt from the 'When Tomorrow Calls'*
series.

If you'd like the prequel to this series ('The Sigma Surrogate') as a gift,
please email me at janita@firefinchpress.com and I'll send it to you.

***

A well-built man in grimy blue overalls waits outside the front door of
a Mr Edward Blanco, number 28, Rosebank Heights. He's on a short
stepladder and is pretending to fix the corridor ceiling light, the bulb
of which he had unscrewed the day before. Just as he knew she would,
the old lady at the end of the passage called general maintenance, the
number which he has temporarily diverted to himself.

He would smirk, but he takes himself too seriously. People in his occupation are often thought of having little brain-to-brawn ratio, but in his

case, it isn't true. You have to be smart to survive in this game, to stay out of the Crim Colonies.

Smart, and vigilant, he thinks, as he hears someone climbing the stairs behind him and holds an impotent screwdriver up to an already tightened screw. The unseen person doesn't stop at his landing.

The man in overalls lowers his screwdriver and listens. He's waiting for Mr Blanco to run his evening bath. If Blanco doesn't start during the next few minutes, he'll have to leave and find another reason to visit the building. He has already been there for twenty minutes, and even the pocket granny would know that you don't need more than half an hour to fix a broken light.

At five minutes left, he rechecks the lightbulb and fastens the surrounding fitting, dusts it with an exhalation, folds up his ladder. As he closes his dinged metal toolbox, he hears the movement of water flowing through the pipes in the ceiling. He uses a wireless device in his pocket to momentarily scramble the entrance mechanism on the door. It's as simple as the red light changing to green, a muted click, and he silently opens the door at 28. In the entrance hall of Blanco's flat, he eases off his workman boots, strips off his overalls to reveal his sleeker outfit of a tight black shirt and belted black pants.

The burn scars on his right arm are now visible. The skin is mottled, shiny. He no longer notices it; it's as much a part of him as his eyes or his nose. Perhaps subconsciously it is his constant reminder why he does what he does. Perhaps not.

He stands in his black stockinged feet, biding his time until he hears the taps being turned off. Mr Blanco is half whistling, half humming. A small man; effeminate.

What is that song? So familiar. Something from the 1990s? No, later than that. Melancholy. A perfect choice, really, for how his evening will turn out.

He hears the not-quite-splashing of the man lowering himself into the bath. Tentative. Is it too hot, or too cold? Or perhaps it's the colour of the water putting him off. Recycled water has a murkiness to it, a suspiciousness. Who knows where that water has been, what it has seen? The public service announcements, now planted everywhere, urge you to shower instead of bath, to save water. It does seem like the cleaner option. If you insist on bathing, they preach, you don't need a depth of more than five fingers. And then, only every second day. His nose wrinkles slightly at that. He takes his cleanliness very seriously.

Mr Blanco settles in and starts humming again. The man with the burnt arm glides over the parquet flooring and enters the bathroom. Even though his eyes are shut, the man in the bath senses his presence, his face stamped with confusion. The scarred man sweeps Blanco up by his ankles in a graceful one-armed movement, causing water to rush up his nose and into his mouth. As he chokes and writhes upside-down, the man gently holds his head under the water with his free hand.

It's a technique he learnt from watching a rerun on the crime channel. In the early 1900s a grey-eyed George Joseph Smith, dressed in colourful bow ties and hands flashing with gold rings, married and killed at least three women for their life insurance. He would prowl promenades in the evenings looking for lonely spinsters and pounce at any sign of vulnerability. His charisma, likened to a magnetic field, ensured the women would do as he told them, one of his wives even buying the bath in which she was to be murdered. His technique in killing them was cold-blooded, clean: he'd grip their ankles to pull their bodies under—submerge them so swiftly that they would lose consciousness immediately—and they would never show a bruise. But where such care had been taken in the actual murders, Smith was careless with originality and was caught and hanged before he could kill another bride in the bath.

A moment is all it takes, and soon Mr Blanco is reclining in the bath again, slack-jawed, and just a little paler than before. The man in black turns on the taps and fills the tub. It turns out five fingers is enough in which to drown, but it would be better if it looks like an accident.

Mr Blanco's face is a porcelain mask, an ivory island in the milky grey water. Perhaps the person who finds him will think he fell asleep in the bath which he has, in a way. The man washes his hands in the basin, wipes down the room. He throws on the white-collared shirt he brought with him, and within five minutes he is out of the building and walking to the bus station, dumping the dummy toolbox and overalls on the way. He hops on a bus just as it's pulling out onto the road. He's in a good mood, but he doesn't show it. This was one of his easier jobs. He wonders if the other six names on the list will be as effortless.

The man slides his hand into his pocket and pulls out the curiosity he lifted from Blanco's mantelpiece: a worn piece of ivory—a finger-polished piano key. Engraved on the underside: 'Love you always, my Plinky Plonky.' It's smooth in his palm and retains the warmth of his skin. A melody enters his head. Coldplay: that's what Blanco was humming. The man finds this very satisfying.

***

The man dressed as a nurse puts his latex-covered fingers on William Soraya's wrist, feels his pulse. It is slow and steady. There is no need to do it: the unconscious athlete is hooked up to all kinds of monitoring equipment. He fusses about the room, rearranging giant bouquets and baskets of fruit and candy. He admires the medal—Soraya's first Olympic gold—on the bedside table. Its placement seems a desperate plea: *You were once the fastest man in the world, you can beat this. Please wake up.*

The man wearing the borrowed scrubs takes what looks like a pen out of his pocket, clicks it as if he is about to write on Soraya's chart, and spikes the tube of the IV with it. It is slow-acting enough to give him the ninety seconds he will need to leave the hospital. No alarms will go off while he is still here. He takes the medal and slips it into his trouser pocket as he moves. It is cold against his thigh.

It's a bitterbright feeling for him, leaving while his mark is still breathing. Doesn't feel right, especially after the accident he engineered hasn't proved to be fatal. Still, there will be others. He walks down the passage as quickly as he can without alerting anyone. He breathes hot air into his medimask, requisite for any doctor, nurse, patient or visitor in the hospital. It's large and covers most of his face, which is most fortunate. Hospitals are one of the easiest places to kill people. His borrowed scrubs cover his other distinguishing characteristics, apart from his generous build, and height. But no one will say: there was a nurse in there with a burnt arm.

***

An attractive platinum-haired woman sits on a park bench at a children's playground in uptown ChinaCity/ Sandton. You can see that she is wealthy. She's laser-tanned, wearing SaSirro top to bottom, some understated white gold jewellery, and has a smooth, unworried forehead, but that's not what gives her wealth away. She is watching the ultimate status symbol: her white pony-tailed son, playing in the sandpit next to the jungle gym. He holds a dirty grey bunny—a stuffed animal—under one arm as he builds a sandcastle with the other. The toy goes everywhere with the boy.

The perfectly made-up woman may look like a bored, stay-at-home mother, but she is in fact on her office lunch break. She was top of her class every year at Stellenbosch University and was fluent in 26 languages by the time she was twenty-one. She didn't finish her degree: she was poached by the top legal attorney firm eight months before she graduated, won over by a huge salary and the promise that she would make partner by twenty-five, which she did.

The woman opens her handbag, takes out a pill, pops it into her mouth and washes it down with a gulp of Anahita, saying a silent prayer for whichever drug company it is that makes TranX. She should know the name—she can tell you the capital city, currency and political state of nearly every country in the world—but today she can't picture the label on the box of capsules in her head. She wonders if she is burnt out; she definitely feels it.

Her son begins a tentative conversation with another little boy in the sandbox. Always the charmer. Her heart contracts; she loves him fiercely, every square millimetre of his skin, every pale hair, every perfect bone, she loves. The scent of his little-boy skin. His cow-licked crown. She has such dreams for him, wonders what he will be like at ten, sixteen, thirty. She never thought she'd feel this way about another person. She'd grown up feeling aloof, alone, her parents blaming it on her stellar IQ, but when her son was born that sad bubble burst. It hasn't taken away her anxiety or depression, but it has given her quiet, exquisite moments of joy she hadn't before imagined possible.

Satisfied that her son is playing happily, she opens her lunchbox. She takes home 32 million rand a year, but she still packs her own lunch every day. Today it is a mango, pepper leaf and coriander salad, humble edamame with pink Maldon salt, and a goose carpaccio and kale poppy-seed bagel.

She takes a few bites of the bagel, enjoying the texture of the expensive meat, the tingling of the mustard. Soon there is a slight tickling at the back of her throat. She tries to swallow the irritation, but it lingers. Trying to stay calm, she opens her bagel and inspects the contents, assuring herself that she had made the sandwich, and that there was no place for contamination. The itch becomes stronger, furring over her tongue too.

She drops the bagel, starts to hyperventilate, presses the panic button on her locket. It sends a request for a heli-vac and a record of her medical history, including her severe peanut allergy, to the nearest private hospital. Her airway is closing now, and she clutches her throat, desperate to keep it open. She searches for her EpiPen, but when she can't see it, looks for a straw, a ballpoint, anything she can force down her throat to keep breathing, but her hands are shaking too much. She loses control over her fingers.

She stands up, lurches forward, waves blindly trying to attract someone's attention. Her vision becomes patchy; there are sparks and smoke clouds blotting out her son. She tries to call him, tries to call anyone for help, but it's too late for that. One arm outstretched towards her son, she sinks to her knees on the grass, blue-faced, and topples over.

A woman's gasp rings out, and concerned strangers come to surround her. Ambulances are called, CPR is administered, but the woman dies within the minute. A white-haired toddler is held back, not kicking and screaming as you'd expect, but dumb with shock.

The strangers stand distraught, arms by their sides, not knowing what to do next. Just terrible. What a tragedy. They begin framing the story in their minds, to tell spouses and friends later. They think of how to word it in their respective status updates. Where is the ambulance? They have children to mind, places to be. One bystander, a large man with a scarred arm, gives up on finding a pulse and walks away. Furtively, he strokes the soft stuffed rabbit he has hidden under his jacket. Chopping of the sky can be heard in the distance: the heli-vac approaching. It forms the intro to the song that starts in his head. He hums along—Pink Floyd?—and doesn't look back.

. . .

***

Betty arrives at work slippery with sweat. She has no option but to run to her grind at Propag8 now that the taxi drivers are trying to kill her. She bought an electric car, but they keep trying to booby-trap it. Every time she puts her thumb on the ignition switch, she closes her eyes and waits for the explosion. Every time the car starts without blowing up, she knows it's just a matter of time. That she has bought one more day. That they are watching her, waiting for the perfect time to detonate her life.

Betty can't handle the daily anxiety, the red-wire-or-black-wire stomach cramps she gets, waiting to be blown to high heaven. Not that she believes in heaven. Not that she believes anything, except the voices in her head.

So she can't drive the car, but she can't sell it either, because that would entail meeting up with someone and giving him her bank details. Even if she trusted banks—which she doesn't—she won't want to give those details out to a stranger. She'll have to drive it to an abandoned shopping mall in Fourways and park it there, wipe it down so that there are no fingerprints. No DNA. Because nowadays if you give someone your dynap code, you may as well just hand them everything you own.

Danger everywhere. Can't drive to work, can't catch a ride, so she has to run. Same thing goes for grocery shopping. No wonder she's lost so much weight. Sometimes when she looks in the mirror, she's shocked by the haunted skeleton that stares back at her. She probably wouldn't even buy groceries if it weren't for her beagle. It's not the first time the dog has saved her life.

Betty uses her wafer key to get into her office, closes the door behind her, and cranks down all the blinds. She pulls out a few hotwipes to remove the sheen of perspiration she feels all over her body. She scrubs her face and under her arms and is about to sit down when a male voice crackles into the room.

"Betty."

She shoots up before her pants even touch the chair.

"Yes?" She's still not used to the disembodied voices of her colleagues beaming into her office like this. As if they're sitting in a control room, like a god, observing her every move. As if she's a cat in a Schrödinger dream.

Is she alive, or dead? She pinches her forearm and welcomes the pain. She's alive. She doesn't know how much longer that'll be true, but today, this minute, she is alive. It won't last long, so it's a bit like being alive and dead at the same time.

She's asked them to refrain from using the Voice Beam in her office, because of her condition, but sometimes they forget. Or maybe they just don't care that she already has enough voices in her head to deal with, without adding staff announcements like *There will be tea and zucchini cake served in the Dahlia Room at* 11:00 and *Please don't forget to lock your desks when you leave for the day,* as if she needs reminding. If there is one thing Betty is good at, it's locking up.

"Betty," repeats the voice.

"Yes!" She looks around the room, expecting to see hundreds of swivelling eyeballs in the ceiling, staring down at her. She imagines the sound they would make, and she shudders.

"Mandla here. Please come to my office."

"Uh oh," whispers Betty. "That doesn't sound good."

She glances at her snakewatch. Yes, she's late for work again. Of course she's late! Her manager would also be late for work every day if he had to run a marathon just to show up. When she'd told Mandla her problem, he had been understanding. He knew her diagnosis, knew she needed to do things her way. He was—mostly—willing to overlook her compelling eccentricities. But now he's called her to his office, and she doubts it's for a promotion.

Betty knocks on his glass door and jumps away as it slides open. Her manager looks up with a ghost of a smile. He motions for her to come inside, and the door closes soundlessly behind her.

"Betty." He's friendly but firm. "Take a seat."

She continues to stand. "You're firing me."

Mandla stops smiling. "I'm sorry."

"I understand. I'm two hours late."

"It's not just about being late. I'm happy to give you the flexitime you need. I just think—"

Betty stares at him. Part of her wants to put him out of his misery, tell him it's okay, she's glad she won't have to run so much anymore, or deal with insensitive colleagues, or taste the awful office decaf again. The other part of her wants him to squirm. She's given most of her adult working life to this place. She's responsible for the most ground-breaking accomplishments they've achieved, and what does she get in return? A simpering idiot telling her she needs to get help. Because that's what he's going to say, isn't it?

"I think you need to focus on getting well. Perhaps some additional treatment for your ... condition."

"What do you know about my *condition*?"

"I know that when I met you, you were the brightest, edgiest biohorti-
culturalist I had ever met. You started programmes here that were
light years ahead of any other seed storage facility in the world."

Betty stares at him. "It doesn't matter, though, does it?"

He hits the desk with his palm, and Betty jumps.

"Of course it matters!" Mandla says, and he seems to mean it. His
expression is tight with regret. He sighs and sits back in his chair,
resigned. "It matters."

Betty stares at him while her voices whisper in her head. She ignores
them.

"You're wrong," she says, and leaves his office.

***

"Come on, girl," Betty says to the beagle she's dragging on her red
lead. The hound's not in a hurry: she's enjoying the impromptu walk,
the companionship, the thousand different scents steaming from the
hot sidewalk. The beagle looks up at Betty, panting, happy, and Betty
softens the line. It's not the dog's fault she's in a hurry. Usually Betty
wouldn't bring her out on a mission like this—it slows her down—but
the beagle started whining and crying when she was getting ready to
leave her flat, which made Betty blanch with guilt. Then she'd felt
some kind of evil, some kind of invasion, and suddenly her home had
looked different—as if someone had come in while she was sleeping
and replaced all her furniture with exact copies. Her favourite wing-
back chair looked like the original, it even had the coffee stain on the
arm, and the dog-claw scratches on the stained timber legs, but Betty
knew it was an imposter. She'd inspected it, even got down on her

bony knees to sniff it—which the beagle had thought was a game and joined in—and even the smell was spot-on. How did they get that right? *These creeps ... these creeps are not to be underestimated. These people are very good at what they do.*

Then she'd noticed the painting on the wall—a landscape by a local artist picked up years ago at the Rosebank Flea Market—looked different, too. The scudding clouds were moodier, and there was something wrong with the shade of the sky.

It's just a matter of time before they get her. Maybe she shouldn't give them the satisfaction. Maybe she should kill herself. It'll be better than waiting around like a sitting duck.

Yes.

That is what she'll do, but first, she has to warn the others. The envelopes tremble in her hand.

After she'd packed up her box of belongings at work and dumped them into the incinerator chute, she'd hidden the list of barcodes—seven barcodes, including hers—in the false bottom of a safety deposit box. There's no safer place than a safety deposit box at a seed bank. Now she has three copies of the wafer key that will open it, along with three identical letters, in three separate envelopes, all for the same person. One to speed-post, one to hand-deliver, and one as a backup, in case the first two are somehow intercepted. She clutches the envelopes, and her perspiration makes the paper turn leathery. The beagle spots some pigeons in the distance and barks, straining at the lead, and Betty jogs along with her, scattering the charcoal-feathered birds as they go.

***

Betty watches from afar as the funeral party leave the building. She's sweating, sweating, always sweating, despite the reprieve from the too-hot sun the tree's shade offers her. Her SPF100 is leaking down her cheeks. One day they'll be playing with the weather and the sun will explode and kill them all.

"What are you doing here?"

The man's terse voice startles her, sending her heart racing even faster than before.

"Holy!" She coughs in shock and knocks at her chest with her white-knuckled fist. "You gave me such a fright."

James doesn't apologise. "You shouldn't be here."

He's wearing a dark suit, an elegant cut.

Betty tries to swallow the dryness in her mouth. A velcro furball of anxiety. "I tried sending Kate the letters. I don't think she's getting them."

"Her name is Kirsten."

"She needs to know."

"No. She needs to be protected from your paranoid delusions."

"Don't you see it? Don't you see what's happening?"

James's jaw muscles flicker under his skin. "Please leave."

"They're closing down the cell!"

James looks around, maybe hoping that no one will see them talking. "I've asked you before to leave us alone—"

"Christ. Can you not hear what I am saying? We're on *the list*. They will kill us all!"

"No," says James, glancing over at the funeral party. "Kirsten's parents were killed in a botched burglary."

Betty chokes. "I know you don't believe that."

She swipes at the sweat that's running down her temples.

"Look," says James. "I know you've been having some ... health issues."

Betty hisses at him through her clenched jaw. "You've been watching me. I *knew* someone was watching me."

"I haven't been. Propag8 made a statement in the *Science Journal*, that's all. Said they have granted you a medical hiatus. Your work is famous, whether you like it or not."

"Don't try to turn this around."

"I'm not. I'm ... offering help."

"You're going to try to bribe me. To keep quiet."

James shakes his head, ruffles his soft blond hair. His eyes arrest hers. "Please, Betty."

"Betty-Barbara," she says. "Kirsten-Kate."

"Kirsten's been through enough. Please don't make this any more diffi-cult than it has to be."

He turns away from her and starts walking back towards the TreePod building.

"How many, James?" she calls after him.

He stops and turns around. Annoyance flashes on his face. "What?"

"How many people will have to die before you pay attention?"

* * *

Betty stands under a silver birch. It's a young tree, recently planted, but it casts enough shade to keep her from the maniacal sun, and the blistering bark is proving interesting enough for her beagle to investigate. It's Betty's first time at CityLeaf. She usually avoids botanical gardens and parks, despite her profession—or, as she has to continually remind herself, her *previous* profession.

Too many strangers; too much open space. It makes her feel so flesh-coloured and vulnerable. A skinned rat. A baby bird thrown out of its nest by a storm. A snail pulled from its shell. How do these other people cope, she wonders, as they skip by her in their athleisure gear and designer superbug masks that match their tin water bottles. How do they not feel the continual oppressive thrust in the atmosphere that threatens to flatten Betty against the ground?

The beagle has sniffed enough of the tree's scent history now, and strains against her leash, almost choking herself, trying to get to the next object to explore. Betty winds the handle of the leather lead tightly around her bony hand.

"Wait," she whisper-scolds, not wanting to give up the shelter of the leaves overhead, or her view. She's watching Kirsten sit on a hover-bench in the kids' playground area. The jungle gym equipment is bright and new, and utterly empty of children. Kirsten hasn't moved in twenty minutes, and her face remains blank. The picture spooks Betty, but she can't tear herself away.

Has Kirsten/Kate received the letter she posted to her? If not, surely she got the one she had pushed under her apartment door?

The dog whimpers, lamenting the trove of lost opportunities just out of her reach. The sound skewers Betty with guilt. She's such a good girl, not much of a guard dog, but loyal to a fault. She bends over to stroke the hound's head, scratches her neck, then digs in her jacket pocket for a bone-shaped biscuit, but comes up empty-handed.

Empty pocket.

Frustrated, Betty sighs and closes her eyes. Kirsten hasn't got any of the letters or the keys. If she had, she wouldn't be sitting in an open park like this, presenting herself as such an easy target. If she'd received one of the envelopes, she would have gone straight to the Doomsday Vault, but Betty knows she hasn't.

She's not received the warnings, and there's no time to send more. Betty will have to approach her directly. This is not what she wanted. The idea makes her sweat, and she wipes the perspiration off her top lip with a bent finger that smells of warm leather and dog skin.

The leaves above her move in the breeze, whispering silver threats. Betty ignores the voices. She has to focus. She has to keep her mind clear.

The way forward is obvious: Betty will have to force her hand.

The beagle strains and lets out a high-pitched whine. When Betty opens her eyes again, Kirsten is gone.

* * *

Betty checks the locks on her door for the fifth time. They're locked, but checking them makes her feel safer. She has to do things that make her feel safer.

She sits in front of her blank homescreen but realises the remote isn't working. Betty shakes the remote around a little, tries again. Then she opens up the back and makes sure the batteries are in place. Takes them out, puts them back in. Still, the glass stays clear. Betty gets up to check its connections and sees it's unplugged. She picks up the plug and moves it towards the wall but stops when she reads an orange sticker covering the electrical outlet and switch: 'Don't watch TV.' It's in her handwriting.

Yes, television is not good for me. She should get rid of the screen, but it was expensive, and she abhors waste. The voices are the reason she can't watch anymore. They tell her to do things. Soap opera stars, talk show hosts, newsreaders. They tell her that creeps are trying to kill her, blow up her building, decimate the country. They make her write letters to people, telling them they are in danger. Politicians, local celebrities, airlines.

The police have been here before. They were rough until she showed them the doctor's note she keeps in her bra. The voices speak directly to her. 'Barbara,' (for they have recently taken to calling her Barbara), 'the next bus you take will be wired with a car-bomb with your name on it.' That's when she stopped taking the bus. The communal taxi and individual cab drivers are also not to be trusted. They could take you anywhere, and you'd never be seen again.

Disappear. She clicks her fingers. *Just like that. Click, click.*

Also, food is a problem. She can't run with all her groceries, so she has to shop every day. She doesn't enjoy shopping: too many people. Her psychologist says to try online shopping. Everyone's doing it, but that will mean giving strangers her address and the hours she will be home. Even if the shop people are harmless, the information could be intercepted.

When she finally builds up supplies, she ends up throwing them away. The fridge door looks suspicious: full of invisible fingerprints as if someone else has opened it. An intruder. She tries to work out exactly which food they have contaminated but can never stop at one item. Once the pineberry yoghurt has been binned, the cheddar looks suspect, after that, the pawpaw, the black bread, the SoySpread, the feta. The precious, innocent-looking eggs, the vegetarian hotdogs, the green mango atchar, the leftover basmati, until it is all discarded and sealed tightly in a black plastic bag. The dumping of each individual item causes her pain; she so hates to fritter. This happens once a week.

Sometimes she needs to check the cupboards, too. Sometimes it's not just the open things in the fridge that may have been tainted. She'll get an idea, a name, in her head, and those things will have to go, too. Last week it was Bilchen—pictures in her head of factorybots polluting the processed food then sealing them in neat little parcels, ready to eat. It's as if someone is shouting at her: Bilchen! Bilchen! Like a branded panic attack. Then she has to check every box and packet in her cupboard and toss everything with the Bilchen logo. Not much is left over.

She chooses a lonely tin of chickpeas, checks the label, and eases it open with an old appliance. She polishes a fork with her tracksuit top and eats directly out of the can. Canned food is relatively safe. She reaches for the kosher salt pebbles, but before she grinds it, she sees the top is loose. She pictures arsenic, cyanide, a sprinkling of a strain of a deadly virus, and puts it back without using it. Washes her hands twice and sprays them with hand sanitiser.

She takes the chickpea can with her and walks around her flat, checking all the windows. She touches the locks as she goes, counting them. Mid-count, she hears a noise. A scraping, a whirring. Is someone trying to get in? Is the front door locked? Icy sweat.

There is a high-pitched squeal at her heels, and Betty jumps in fright. Her beagle scurries away from her with hurt in her eyes.

'Oh, I'm sorry,' she says, moving to hug and pet her. 'I'm so sorry, my girl. There's a good girl. There's a good girl.' The words soothe them both.

Sometimes if she talks loudly enough to herself, she can drown out the voices. Not in public, though. She shouldn't talk to herself in public. She doesn't like being in public anymore. Sometimes she has to show people the note; she doesn't like that, the look in their eyes.

Squatting on the ground, she feeds the dog some chickpeas. She'll start the counting again.

Outside the door to her apartment, there is humming. A large man in overalls is polishing the parquet corridor. When he moves beneath the glow of the lightbulb, you can see a shiny burn scar on his arm.

9

CHICKEN MATH

"You're crazy," said my husband, his eyes twinkling with a mixture of amusement and confusion. My boss had the same expression just days before when I turned down his offer of a promotion; one that would mean a significant jump in income. The new job title would come with more responsibility, more client meetings, and worst of all: more management of people. Longer hours, more extended conversations. My anxiety level was high enough, thank you very much.

"I'm not crazy," I said to my husband, John. "I'm obsessed. There's a difference."

The week before, I had been an up-and-coming chartered accountant in the most well-regarded financial institution in the country. Now I would be trapped in the purgatory that comes with being a woman unwilling to rise to the heady temptation of the success ambition brings.

"It's not the life I want," I told my boss, who was baffled by my decision.

"What do you want?" He seemed genuinely interested.

The problem was, I didn't know.

I knew I didn't want children, and I didn't want to get married—I made an exception for John because he's the best person I ever met. I wanted enough money to be comfortable, but not so much that I felt guilty or wasteful. I didn't need the latest fashion or designer kit. I cut and colour my own hair, much to my friends' horror.

What do you want? my boss had asked. The fact that I didn't know perplexed us both.

I had been a go-getter in school, but it changed when I entered university. My time there turned my life on its head, and I was happy to be relegated to the quiet corner where the rest of the shadows gathered.

"You want what?" asked my husband, when, after some soul-searching, I broke the news.

"Chickens," I said. I knew it sounded ridiculous. We lived in a suburb in one of the craziest cities in the world. I had no business wanting to keep chickens.

"Chickens," he said, as if saying it out loud would make me laugh and tell him I was kidding.

"Just a couple. They're wonderful pets. Apparently." Of course, I had zero experience of the birds. I liked the shape of them, and the way they looked when they walked, and that was about the extent of my wisdom. John threw his head back and laughed, but not in an unkind way. Still, it took some convincing. I agreed to do all the work and pay for all the expenses. He'd get beautiful fresh eggs and some new pets who had a silly walk. It's called chicken TV—just being outside and watching the chickens—and if you add a G&T to the mix, you may as well be on holiday.

I had an answer for each objection.

. . .

They cluck. Dogs bark louder.

The neighbours will be unhappy. We will give them farm fresh eggs.

They will destroy the garden. They eat aphids for breakfast! Literally!

They cost money to feed. Chickens turn kitchen scraps into pure, healthy protein. No wonder there is the story about the golden goose. They are genuinely miraculous creatures.

They poo everywhere. It's great fertiliser.

I'm not an idiot (most of the time). I knew chickens weren't the answer to my existential crisis. But just thinking about them made me feel better about the world. It was easy to feel bludgeoned by the news headlines; men attacking women in every way: their rights, their bodies, their state of mind. Corporations burning the planet. How is one supposed to get out of bed in the mornings? I would get chickens, and a beehive, and a cow to milk. (Only joking about the cow.) I would plant a vast vegetable garden for us to share, and I would give as much food as I could to people who needed it. For once, since that varsity incident, I had the energy to start a new project. Before I had even really planned it, I had converted the unused garden shed we had inherited with the house and refurbed it. I got out the power drill and attached chicken wire to the window frames, to keep the genets out. I dragged branches I found two blocks away from my house into the coop as perches and made a forest floor for them from dry leaves and rosemary cuttings. John fenced off the area around the coop for the chicken run, and we were in business! The chicken business, to be precise.

We agreed that if we were going to get two chickens, we might as well get three. My chicken contact tried to sell me a tray of twenty-five chicks. Finally, it was my turn to tell someone they were crazy. It made a nice change.

Instead of being an insta-mom to over two dozen peepers, I tracked down a farmer in a rural area ninety minutes north of the city. The drive was transformative. I was go-getting again. I was in charge of my destiny. I was getting my chickens.

There's a thing called "chicken math." It's when you go shopping for three hens and come home with eight. Not only is it common, it's almost expected. I came back with five hens and three chicks, and I was in love with them. I stroked the hens and fed them lovingly, and was rewarded with an egg on the first morning. It was so fresh it was still warm. Yes, I did wash my hands after collecting it.

Chickens are wonderful creatures. Distant relatives of velociraptors, these feathered dinosaur birds will cheerfully and efficiently peck a smaller creature to death, and they have no hangups around cannibalism. Behind their meek feathered exteriors, they are fierce.

Despite my insistence that hens were relatively quiet creatures, John happened to be home the first time Cinnamon, our Rhode Island Red hen, saw our tabby cat, Laila. She let out an almighty "PA-KAAAAAAAAK!" and Laila bolted. Imagine being a cat and seeing a chicken for the first time? Terrifying and wondrous. John tried to get Cinnamon to hush, but it was no use. She wanted the whole block to know she'd just spotted a small tiger in our garden. I couldn't help feeling little sparks of joy when I watched them bob around.

The chicks were little golden feather dusters on stilts. Silly and sweet. I put smooth stones in their water to prevent them from drowning and secured the top to stop the cats from swiping them. My clever husband rigged up a thermostat-controlled heated room to keep them at the right temperature to thrive. I cuddled them at night, letting them burrow into my neck. Sometimes I'd hold their fragile feathered body in my hand, just firmly enough to make them feel safe, and it would work like hypnosis. Within seconds their eyes would close, and they'd nap in my palm. John, unused to having chickens in our bed, joked that he could imagine in a few months' time when they were fully-grown hens and still in our bed for their night-time cuddle. I laughed so much. It felt good.

They squeaked and peeped all day, but when I turned their light off at bedtime, they fell silent. I slept two meters from their room. During the day, I'd rush home for my lunch hour and sit in the garden with them while they free ranged, pecking at the soil and bathing in the sand. I felt I could watch them for hours. I had always thought I'd make a terrible mother, but being with the chicks made me realise I probably wouldn't be too bad.

I invited my best friend over and told her to bring her son, Damon.

"He'll love the chicks," I said.

She laughed. "I'll love the chicks!" They brought chicken treats over: mixed grain, comfrey, and a spinning cabbage ball.

"You shouldn't have," I said.

"Are you kidding? I finally had an excuse to buy a spinning cabbage ball!"

We settled on a blanket in the garden while the hens milled about, pulling earthworms out of the soil and clucking. When Damon came outside, he got so excited he sprinted to the coop.

"Don't run," I said. "You'll scare them."

He slowed to a jog and crashed into the coop, trying to get hold of one of the hens.

"Can I pick them up?" asked the seven-year-old.

"Um..." I said.

"No, darling," said Brenda.

"He can," I said. "I pick them up. They're happy to be stroked."

Damon cornered Pepper and hugged her to his chest, beaming. I hoped she wouldn't peck him, but at the same time, I thought perhaps it wouldn't be a bad thing for him to learn that you can't just go storming into a hen house without getting some kind of comeuppance. The chicken shared none of my harshness; she looked comfortable in Damon's arms and cooed happily. I snapped a picture for Brenda.

We sat drinking gin and tonics while Damon played with the hens. When it was warm enough to bring the chicks out, they immediately scampered for cover under the jasmine hedge. We managed to gently extricate two, one for Brenda to hold, and one for her son. The chick perched on her hand and fluffed her feathers, and my heart melted. How precious these moments were.

Out of the corner of my eye, I saw Damon running after the other chick as it flapped away from him. I frowned and glanced down at the one on Brenda's hand. When I looked up again, time stopped. Damon was standing there, holding a motionless chick. The lawn was electric green.

"Wait," I said. "What happened?"

The baby had been flapping its wings just seconds before.

"Nothing," he said, shrugging. I took the chick from him and searched for movement, searched for breath. There was none.

"What happened?" I asked again.

"Nothing," he said. "It's just sleeping."

"She's not sleeping," I said. Her fading body was still warm. Her head lolled. The world stood still as the horrible truth rained down on me.

"Her neck's broken," I said.

"You should take it to the vet," said the boy.

I didn't look at him. Couldn't.

Brenda was horrified. Layers of emotion vied for my attention, running together like paint. My heartbreak for the bird, who was only two weeks old. Sympathy for my friend, who began to weep. Empathy for Damon, for he was just a little boy, after all, who didn't understand how fragile chicks were. It's a difficult thing to process, that you've just snuffed out a life. I worried about the consequences for him.

At the same time, I couldn't help but draw the parallel between what had just happened and the latest news headlines. The stories about the men who were intent on taking women's rights and claiming ownership of their bodies in so many different ways. Legally, spiritually, physically. I couldn't help seeing little boys chasing down animals for their pleasure and not giving the animals' feelings a thought. It was all about what they wanted, their own desire. And then a boy snaps a chick's neck and what do we do? We feel sorry for the boy.

"It was an accident," I told him, ruffling his hair. "I know you wouldn't hurt an animal on purpose."

In university, the victim of the unheeded desire was me. Another student chased me down and snapped my neck. At least, that's what it felt like. After he'd satisfied himself, I was the one motionless and fading. I was the one dying from sheer shame. I decided that shadows were good places to hide from rough boys. I was wrong, and was sought out over and over again. It turned out that the shadows made fertile hunting ground for damaged boys. By then, I was so deeply entrenched I didn't know how to get out.

. . .

Brenda arrived the next day with swollen eyes that matched mine. She also brought flowers, gin, and four new chicks—the magic of chicken math.

"Do you still love me?" she asked, eyes shining.

"I'd still love you if you burnt down my entire house," I said.

Spending time with the chicks hopping on and off my lap healed my heart. Over time, my vegetable garden became prolific and gave me peace. The bees made rosemary flavoured honey. John and I sat holding hands while we watched chicken TV, and I realised how wrong I was when I thought that chickens would not be the answer to my decade-old distress. They had scratched the soil and life had bloomed, and I didn't feel as if I was in the shadows anymore.

10

MY FRIDGE IS EMPTY

I DON'T REMEMBER our wedding anniversaries anymore

my husband doesn't hold it against me

I have ante-retrograde amnesia from a knock on the head

I can remember five minutes ago

five seconds

sometimes I have flashbacks of older memories

but not often

not today

Today is toast cold with butter and a small white cat

his tag says Felix

his bowl is full so I think I have fed him this morning

but now I see the sun is setting

the fridge is empty

I will go shopping if I remember

I don't like going out

too much to worry about

I can still drive but I lose my car in the parking lot

I lose my money if I don't keep it in a purse around my neck

purse and a panic button

Did Jack give me the panic button?

I can't remember

I walk outside and see the moving sun on the dark dew grass

Is it morning again?

It was evening just a moment ago and I don't remember sleeping

The newspaper says it's 2019 which can't be right

I got a knock on my head so I don't remember everything anymore

I remember Jack and the babies and when I see the white cat I remember him

I feed him and he purrs

does he belong to me?

Or do I belong to him?

I prefer a world where people belong to cats instead of the other way around

my car is gone but I need to go shopping

the fridge is empty

Felix's bowl is empty

I pressed the panic button and pray someone will arrive

What is wrong asks the woman wearing the sky

my car is gone I need to go shopping

My fridge is empty

You don't have a fridge says the woman

You don't need a fridge

I need food for Felix I say

Who is Felix she asks

My white cat

Felix died dear heart

I begin to cry and I know it's not the first time I've cried for Felix

you had a knock on the head says the woman

don't be hard on yourself

you are doing well

you're getting better

it doesn't feel like it I say

can I have my car keys I ask

I need to get to the shops

yes love says Jack and hands me the keys

feed Felix on your way out

Then I remember it was Jack

who hit me on the head

But when I turn to look at him he's gone.

11

SHELLFIRE & BIRDSONG

12TH FEBRUARY 1916

My love—

France is hell. You wouldn't recognise it; it's nothing like those pretty postcards on your wall. I'm not saying I don't want to be here. I'm proud to serve my country and to keep you safe, and apart from that, there is also the adventure that it is to be here with the boys, like playing an exciting game. I wouldn't want to miss it, even though it is truly terrible at times. Sometimes it is as simple as this: I have a job to do, and I'm here to do it. At other times it is less clear-cut. We are killing men, men that could be us, our friends and brothers, just depending on which side of the line you're standing. And who draws that line, anyway? These are the murky thoughts that come to me in the early hours of the morning when I'm trying to stay warm and awake in the trench that is both my protection and my prison. If nothing else, I have learnt that there is no good or evil, black or white. Just overlapping shades of both and neither, at the same time. Forgive me for rambling, dear heart. I have not slept much, and it is as ever a relief to tell you these things. The men don't understand these things as you do. You are my lighthouse in this roiling storm. You keep me safe and focused, and I love you very much. I may not survive this whole war, but I will stay alive to see you again because that idea has become my shining light. Your light will guide me home.

I love you.

Frederick

PS. I have enclosed a packet of apple seeds for you. We rarely get fresh fruit around here, but when we marched through Calais on arrival, the villagers cheerfully handed us yard-long loaves and some wine and fruit. When I tasted the apple, I thought of you—the bitterness of missing you, the sweetness of the memories I have of you. The seed-star of the core made me imagine planting an apple tree with you and watching it grow along with the children we will one day have, and life will be good.

24th March 1916

My love—

When I am cold and dark, I think of you. It is my sole comfort in a time of pain and uncertainty; not knowing when the next storm of bullets will arrive. I dream of our bed at home and wish we were in it together. I'd wrap my arms around you and warm your skin with mine. My body aches, my skin craves yours. If I could give you my warmth, I would. I would give it all to you and more. Soon the war will be over, and these silly dreams of mine will come true. Visions of us sitting on the porch in the sunshine, dreams of cradling a little baby—will we have a son or a daughter?—dreams of peace and silence and warmth and good simple food. Oh, God! I have never before realised how a simple moment like that could be pure perfection. When I return, we shall have what we both crave, body and mind. I shall survive this war and will come home to you, and we shall have our perfect moments.

Love you

Frederick

2nd June 1917

My love—

You'd be impressed by my new skills here. I'm not referring to stripping down a Vickers machine gun or driving tanks—although I'd like to show you that, too—but I have learnt to cook, and clean, and sew buttons. Everything my mother used to do for me. The boys here say that the war has taught them how to be "men" and I'm sure a particular part of that is inevitable, although I think their definition of "men" may be slightly different to mine and yours. These men just do what they are told; they are not taught to think for themselves. If you were to think for yourself in a war like this ... well, perhaps there wouldn't even be a war at all. But as it stands, I think you wouldn't be able to pick me out from a line-up. We're all identical here, same uniforms, same horse-clipper shaven heads. Thinking for yourself is not encouraged.

I think back now to the days we were in training. Do you remember how I complained about the early wake-ups, and PT, and only one rasher of Lance Corporal Bacon on our breakfast bread? I lamented the fact there was only plum and apple jam — what a boy I was; nothing but a child. I wasn't able to darn my clothes then. I was horrified by having to piss in my army boots to soften them up. But now I know what real horror is; it's when you feel good about taking another man's life. They say that war makes a man out of a boy, but I think the opposite. The shameful truth is that I feel like a scared little boy when I run and stab someone with my bayonet. Perhaps I am just weak and not meant for war.

I'll sign off before I make you feel maudlin.

I do love you.

Fred

15th August 1917

My love—

You may hear stories of soldiers being brave and happy, see pictures of them waving at the camera and sipping from their steaming tin mess cups. But mostly we are overwrought and ill, and I fear this war is damaging me in every way.

I am not writing this to worry you. You are the only one I can tell, and I am desperate to feel close to you.

All my love,

Frederick

21st September 1917

My love—

Do not waste your energy worrying about me. I will fight my way through this for you and because of you. We will have our perfect moments on the porch. We will have our babies and be glad they are safe from the danger that lurks in our enemies.

There is shellfire all day long, which burrows into one's mind and heart. It is not an easy way to live. At first, I tried to imagine it was birdsong, but it was easier, in the end, to accept it for what it was: a constant barrage of projectiles meant to kill us.

The French trenches are like a maze, and it's easy to get lost. We sleep on sandbags and wear dead men's coats on cold nights. Our world is divided by no-man's-land beyond which the Gerries camp. They are like bogeymen because you know if they see you they will kill you. When you look through the periscope, all you see are hundreds of shell holes, our barbed wire, and the German barbed wire. Dead bodies hang on the wire until they're rotten enough to slip off. It's one of the most desolate things I've seen. It's eerie because you never see a sign of life, but you know there are hundreds of men there, within shooting range, ready to put a bullet in you.

There are signs all over the trenches: Piccadilly Circus and Regent Street and that sort of thing, showing you where water was available and where the dangerous parts are—where the German snipers can get you. A bullet can get through a sandbag, so even when you're crouching down in the mud, there's still a chance of getting hit. We spend four days in the line, and then we swap. "Give our love to Gerry," the men joke as they see you off.

It's difficult to sleep and difficult to stay awake. I dug a side in the trench I was guarding last time, and that worked well to keep out of the water. Tea helps you stay awake. The first thing you do when you get to the line is to make a cuppa. The Vickers is a water-cooled gun, so if you fire a few shots, the water boils. Then you disconnect the tube and brew a cup of tea.

We keep our water in petrol cans. Unfortunately, you can taste it in the brew.

If you make a fire to boil water, you use the smallest pieces of wood you can find, even if you're freezing. If the Gerries see smoke, they'll know where to toss their hand grenade. Once you've had your tea, you save a sip to shave with. We go for weeks without washing, and some men are chatty with lice. I run my clothes over a flame, and I can hear their eggs popping. I'm sure you must find that disgusting, but it's quite satisfying, really. I'm always happy to get rid of the buggers; they itch like hell.

We eat tinned stew and bully beef. We eat bread. There never seems to be enough food for us all, but no one complains.

The worst thing about trench duty is hearing the continuous shelling. It sets my heart thundering. It's nerve-wracking and never stops. I think I will hear the whizzing and explosions in my dreams for years to come.

Tell me if this is too much for you, my darling. I don't want to give you nightmares, but it is a relief to tell you what happens here.

I love you.

Fred

11th November 1917

My love—

I will tell you about our future. At first, I thought I'd return home tanned, strong, unhurt, and ready to sweep you into my arms. Now, less naïve, I dream of you tending to me and cooking for me until I am strong enough to start our new life together, and then it will be my turn to tend to you, and tend to you I will. I shall wash your hair as I did during our short engagement; I shall mend your clothes; I shall cook for you. I will never take you for granted.

Frederick

2nd December 1917

My love—

I can picture us under our apple trees, and I shall weave a crown for you made of wildflowers. I don't think you can imagine how very much I love you. How wonderful it is to think of sunshine when here it is so wet and cold. When our boots fill with water it freezes and then you can't get them off. The frostbite is unbearable. The water first covered our boots, then our belts, now it is up to our chests. We try not to complain because even frozen feet are better than trench foot. If you get gangrene, you're simply sent down the line to get your legs hacked off. Sorry, there's no prettier way to say it.

They say here that a man's rifle is his best friend. Mine is a Lee-Enfield, an excellent rifle indeed, a sturdy one. In the beginning, we had to keep our buttons polished and complained we were given nothing to clean them with (we used our toothbrushes). No one shines buttons anymore. We're a rag-tag army now, isolated and despairing that this hell will never end.

I saw a boy die yesterday. He slipped into the sucking slime—that's what we call the sour mud here that's full of decaying bodies and rats—and he just got pulled under. There was nothing we could do to help him, and it was horrifying to watch. Another nightmare to add to my collection, like jam jars on a shelf.

3rd February 1918

My love—

I hope you are getting my letters. I admit it is a difficult thing for me when I don't receive a reply from you. I lie awake worrying for your life and your affections.

They give us a rum ration every morning in an 18-pounder shell cap protector. It's the size of an egg cup. We get forty cigarettes every fort-night; I swap my woodbines for food. I am eternally hungry. Smoking is soothing, but my body craves food. We drink cold peppery pea soup from cans and eat biscuits furred over with green mould. They don't taste too bad.

Love

Frederick

27th August 1918

My love—

I have been ordered to the front line and told in no uncertain terms that we will not be returning home. My feelings are mixed up. I am as scared as all hell of dying—of course I am—scared to become these swollen bodies that boil in swamps around us here, tainting everything, even our petrol tea. I'm fit and young. I'm healthy despite the conditions here. I don't want to die.

There are other feelings, too. I feel bitter about being cheated out of the life we were going to have together. But there is also sweetness—I think of that sunshine porch and the dappled shade of the French apple trees. I think of resting my head in your lap and twining our fingers together as you look down on me, your hair a halo around your face. This is the picture I'll have in my mind when I go down; my last thoughts will be warm and wonderful because they will be of you. How I wish for one last moment with you.

As I sit here on the fire step, I will bid you farewell, hoping to meet you in the time to come if there is a hereafter. Know that my last affectionate thoughts were of you. You have been the best of wives, and I love you deeply. The only one I ever loved. The one who made a man of me. Know that my last thoughts were of you.

Sincerely

Frederick

11th November 1918

My love—

There was a huge poster. "All hostilities will cease on the Western Front at 11 o'clock on the 11th of November 1918." We said to each other—*what day is it?* And someone discovered it was November the 11th! We got shined up, all ship-shape and Bristol fashion. There weren't any cheers or celebrations as the clock reached 11. The noise of gunfire just faded, like thunder. It was so quiet, all I heard were my ears ringing. We were so dazed that we could stand up straight, in the sunshine, and no one would shoot at us.

I hope you don't find me too changed, for I only love you more.

Frederick

13th November 1918

My love—

We are marching out of France, and I'll be home by Tuesday. I have decided to bury all these letters I never posted, along with the apple seeds, on my way. My hope is that the seeds will grow into beautiful trees and provide shelter and sustenance for someone who needs it. I hope they will touch someone one day, the way you touched me. Your memory kept me alive during the most brutal of times. There is a tragedy in that you shall never grow old, but perhaps an orchard will grow, after all.

I love you with my whole being, and more.

Eternally yours

Frederick

12

HONEYTRAP

I was tidying our home office, humming the soundtrack of the new peculiar and confusing game show I had been watching that morning on my phone while I waited for my soba to cook. I was singing—tunelessly—and dancing a bit. What can I say? Even tidying can be fun if you're in a good mood. I like to use the magic feather duster I ordered online. It was from one of those companies that sell everything from tattoo guns to bizarre satin banana-themed underwear—and it only cost two hundred yen—so my expectations were low. But it's great! It's the best duster I have ever used! It is coloured like a rainbow, and it shimmies when you clean. If you get out of bed on the wrong side, it will definitely cheer you up. And not only does it look very neat, but it works really well, too. It traps the dust like no one's business. You must see the dust that comes out of this thing when I shake it out after a day of cleaning! It's like a dust storm has arrived in Tokyo. I tell everyone about it; I love it. I hope the company still manufactures the product. I should check. Maybe they make different colours and shapes. Possibly there will be a unicorn one. Unicorns are so popular right now; I see them on the streets. Stickers, toys, balloons, cakes. Unicorns everywhere. Who would have guessed? It's a wonder anyone in Tokyo is depressed when you see unicorns and glitter everywhere you look.

So I was dusting and shimmying, and I found a box of old gadgets at the top of the long cupboard. My wife, Amaya, is taller than me, so it would have been easy for her to reach, but I had to stand on my office chair to get to it. Now, standing on a chair with wheels isn't the brightest idea, but I was lucky and came away unscathed and with all my vital organs in working order. Not everyone can say that, right? It's another reason to be happy.

The box didn't have too much to cheer about. Some old DVDs, a dust devil, and a flash drive in the shape of a pink and red Hello Kitty®.

"Why, Hello there, Kitty," I said, taking her out of the box. I could tell she hadn't been used very often because the plastic was shiny and the pink lanyard was clean. I was in the middle of cleaning the room, and I didn't want to lose momentum, so I put the drive aside and continued my work. But I hope you won't be disappointed to hear that after a while my curiosity got the better of me. I had never seen this adorable thing before, and I couldn't help wondering where she came from, and what data, if any, she contained in her round belly. I put down the rainbow dust trap, switched on the kettle, and flipped open my laptop. While I mixed some matcha and homegrown honey, I slid Hello Kitty®'s legs into my USB port and waited. The aroma of the tea was delicious, and I couldn't wait to drink it. I was blowing on it too hard, I think, because one moment the tea was in the cup, and the next it was steaming all over my keyboard. I thought I saw a zap of short-circuiting electricity under the keys, and before I even reached for a towel, the laptop had died a short and (hopefully) painless death. That was not ideal, but worse things have happened! Luckily it was not the end of the world. It was an old laptop and needed replacing, anyway. It was good because I'd now be able to get a new computer, which I had wanted for a while. Good things come to those who wait! Even if the drive turned out to be empty, it had brought me luck. I was grateful to hot matcha tea and Hello Kitty®!

. . .

I still had no idea if there was anything on the stick, and I really wanted to find out. Something had gotten into me; a fiery energy emerged from my curiosity. I felt like I would do whatever it took to find out what was on it. I decided I'd go immediately to buy my new laptop. Usually, I'd order it online. I enjoy buying things online and then they arrive at your front door like magic. *Ding-dong! Your magic is here!* But I felt impatient and decided I wanted to go out, anyway. It would be good to get out. I'd buy my new machine and then grab something light for lunch from a street vendor. I like supporting vendors. They stand out there all day cooking for people like me, chopping spring onions and chillies and sweating over boiling noodles. It's not an easy job, and I like to show them my appreciation with a tip. They say *no, no, you're a loyal customer, no need to tip*, but I just smile. I always get extra toppings so it's the least I can do!

The people at the computer shop were accommodating, and I walked out with a new, bigger, better, sleeker laptop. I promised myself there and then as I paid for it I would never drink anything while working on it—not until I was due another upgrade. By then, I was itching to see what was on the Hello Kitty® stick, so I went straight home again to get to know my new machine. By evening, it was all set up. Just then, I heard a rustle at the door, and it opened. I startled, belly burning as if my wife had caught me doing something illicit, and quickly shoved the flash stick into my pocket and plastered a fake smile on my face.

"Amaya-chan!" I said, getting up from perching at the kitchen counter and hugging her.

She smiled and put her handbag down. "Daiki!"

We hugged, and then she washed her hands and began preparing dinner. I offered to chop the onions—Amaya hates chopping onions— and I busied myself with that while struggling to forget about the stick in my pocket. Why had I hidden it from my beloved? I had never kept a secret from her in my life. Something silly in my head was telling me she would be upset if she saw the thing.

"How was tea with Sakura?" I asked.

"Good!" she smiled, tossing the greens into the pan that was spitting with sesame oil. I caught a whiff of *sake* on her breath, which was unusual. Sakura was Amaya's best friend from school. They'd often spend time together—they'd visit once a week at the least—and Amaya always seemed to come back in a good mood. Throughout dinner, the disk burned in my pocket.

At midnight I crept out of bed and into the office. Amaya was sleeping soundly, so it was the perfect time to execute my plan. I would check the disk, put it back in the box at the top of the tall cupboard, and then go to sleep and forget about it. That stinging feeling in my stomach was back as if my body knew I had a shameful secret inside, even though I did not. My new laptop started beautifully, and I finally slid the Hello Kitty® into the port. There was only one folder, called Daiki Tanaka. My name. I clicked it open.

I didn't understand the contents of the file. The sub-folders were called 'Hobbies'; 'Books'; 'Movies'; 'Music', and 'Miscellaneous'. They contained lists of my favourite things. Also, my birthday, star sign, and pictures of me as a child and teen, and even one at graduation. Who would have compiled these lists and collected these photographs? I didn't understand. How did they get the baby pictures? As far as I knew, the only place they existed was in my parents' family album. Hearing a movement from our bedroom, I quickly whipped the drive out and slung it in my drawer, shutting the laptop. When I climbed back into bed, my feet were cold, and I couldn't sleep. Looking at the data had just made me more curious, not less. What on earth was that about?

Usually, when I can't sleep, I count my blessings. It's like counting sheep, but more fun. Amaya was always top of that list. I knew how fortunate I was to have her. When I got to 35 years old, my parents began to nag me to settle down. I didn't even have a girlfriend, and they wanted grandchildren! Amaya appeared as if in a honey-flavoured dream. I was attending a beekeeping workshop, and she happened to sit next to me. I quickly read her name tag and then looked away as not to appear inappropriate. She was so beautiful that I started to sweat. When she smiled at me, I blushed and felt idiotic. I had never been very good with women. Some friends of mine were always talking to girls, but I never knew what to say. Amaya had long, flowing dark hair and a complexion of fresh snow. Her name means "Night Rain". I remember thinking how perfect it was for her. Eventually, I gathered enough courage to greet her. I loosened my collar and cleared my throat.

"You like bees?" I asked, rather pathetically.

Amaya giggled.

"Sorry," I said, my cheeks turning a deeper shade. "Stupid question."

"Yes," she said, smiling with perfect teeth. "I like bees."

"Do you have a hive at home?"

She shook her head. "I'd love to, but my place is so small. I don't have a garden. There's no space for bees."

"I have one," I said.

Amaya sat up. "You do?"

"I caught a swarm last year and transferred them from the catch box to the hive in September. I've already had honey from them."

"That's wonderful," Amaya said.

That's when I noticed the tiny gold pendant on her necklace. It was a bee set against a hexagonal frame. I gulped. It was now or never. "You could come to see it if you like."

"Are you crazy?" she asked, her eyes wide.

"Sorry," I said, flustered, my damp hands dancing on my lap. "My apologies. You don't want to visit a random stranger. I—"

"I didn't mean that," she said. "I meant, are you crazy? I'd love to see them!"

That beekeeping workshop changed my life. I genuinely think I'd still be single and lonely if I hadn't met Amaya that day. Sometimes I call her my delicious honeytrap. After a whirlwind courtship, we married, and my parents could not have been happier. They seemed to like Amaya as much as I did. Unfortunately, my bride's parents had passed away when she was younger, but my mom and dad treated her like a daughter. Even today, my mother brings over treats for her every week, perhaps hoping to fatten her up to get ready for babies.

"We're not ready for kids yet!" I fibbed to my mom. I was ready; it was Amaya who seemed reluctant.

"Not ready? Nonsense!" replied Mom. "If you wait too long, you'll run out of energy."

I didn't agree; I had always had plenty of energy. Energy was never a problem. But I took her point. I didn't want to get to the point where I needed a walking stick to attend our kids' soccer games. When I brought it up with Amaya, her answer was always the same.

I'm not ready yet. Maybe next year.

It was her body, and I respected that. I'd never want to pressure her into anything.

. . .

I called Sakura the next day, hoping to get an idea for a birthday gift for Amaya. I was fresh out of inspiration. I had the bad habit of buying her presents all year round, so when important occasions came up, I had nothing in the closet for her.

"Any chance that Amaya mentioned anything yesterday?" I asked. "About something she's fond of lately?"

"Yesterday?" asked Sakura. "I think you've got your wires crossed."

"Amaya said she had tea with you."

There was an awkward silence on the line. Sakura's voice got smaller, and she said, "Oh."

"You didn't see her?" I asked.

"I haven't seen her in a few weeks," said Sakura. "She's been busy."

I was confused because I knew for a fact that Amaya had kissed me goodbye and left to see Sakura twice the week before. I felt sick. This time it was my turn to say *Oh*.

The next time Amaya was due to meet with "Sakura", I tagged along. By that, I mean I followed her at a safe distance. She didn't act suspiciously at all, except when she climbed out of a taxi outside a tower of apartments I didn't recognise. Standing there, she quickly looked left and right, perhaps to see if there was anyone who would recognise her, and wonder why she was going into a strange building. But she needn't have worried, because Tokyo is such a busy place; the kind of place you can disappear if you want to. She went inside the building, and I followed. I thought I might lose her if she disappeared into the elevator, but she strode into the restaurant on the ground level. I didn't go inside. I stood behind a tall ficus and watched her walk to a reserved table, and I wished like anything that Sakura would soon arrive, and I could sigh and leave swiftly. That did not happen.

A well-dressed man in a dark grey suit arrived and sat opposite her, and they immediately fell into what looked like a lively conversation, which lasted an hour. My heart began to ache. It would be so terrible, so very terrible to lose Amaya. We were perfect for each other! We both loved milkshakes, Rocky Balboa, bees, football, and shirataki. I loved her without limits; my parents thought of her as a daughter. I couldn't lose her, but I didn't know what to do. Some men would fly into a rage—some would hurt their wives—but that was the last thing I wanted to do. Violence was the opposite of how I was feeling. I stood behind that plant for an hour, feeling as if I was losing my wife with every minute that passed. My only consolation was that they didn't touch or kiss. It was cold comfort.

That night Amaya wrapped her slender arms around me and asked me what was wrong.

"You're not yourself," she said.

"I'm all right," I told her, turning away to hide my wretchedness. "Just a headache."

She made me ginger tea with our homemade honey to soothe the pain, but it did not help.

The next meeting with "Sakura" took us to a wedding of a young couple where I had to camouflage myself behind a draped pillar while I watched the guests file into the chapel. Amaya looked radiant in a modest blue dress I recognised. When she took the arm of yet another stranger, I felt like she had stabbed me in the heart. Although they were not intimate, it was clear she was attending the wedding as the man's date. I didn't know if it would hurt more to see her with the restaurant man again or if a new face was worse. My mind was swirling, and I didn't know what to think. I wanted to tell someone. I realised that Amaya was my best friend because usually, I told her everything. Now, when I really needed her, I had no one. I didn't want to trouble my parents, and I had no siblings. Sleeping became difficult, and I lost my normally healthy appetite. The street vendors called out at me as I passed them.

"Hey, Daiki-san" they yelled, grinning. "Was it something we said?"

I bought a pancake to reassure them and fed it to a stray dog on the next block.

The next time I had trouble sleeping, I took Amaya's phone and searched it. We both knew each other's passwords, so it was easy to get in. I flipped through her photos, her notes, her social media, and found nothing unusual. She didn't have any new contacts that I didn't know which puzzled me further. Surely if she were seeing other men, she'd have their numbers and some messages from them? But Amaya was too bright for that, I realised. If she were having affairs, she wouldn't keep any evidence on her phone. Not the phone I knew the password to, anyway. I switched on a flashlight and began combing through her cupboard while she slept. I felt guilty doing it, but I was desperate to know what was going on. While my nature is usually extremely optimistic, I found myself suspecting the worst. Just before I was about to give up searching for her secret phone, I heard a vibration deep in the closet. Like the flash drive, it was high up and pushed right towards the back, hidden in a pair of black socks. I extricated it and looked at the alien device in my hand. I hesitated, getting the feeling that it was a digital pandora's box. Once I looked at what was on the phone, there'd be no going back.

I made sure that Amaya was sound asleep before I held the biometric button to her thumb to unlock the phone, then I took it to the bathroom and closed the door. I was holding my breath as I scrolled through the list of contacts. I didn't recognise one name of the hundreds listed; mostly male, some female. One of the contact numbers was the name of a bank we did not bank with, along with what I guessed was an account number and PIN. I looked for the bank app on the phone and logged in with that information. My stomach cramped when I saw the account information. Why did my wife have a secret bank account? Did I not give her enough money to live comfortably? And, why was there only one benefactor listed on the statement for every single payment to her?

THE FAMILY ROMANCE OF NEUROTICS

I spent the night with the odd name bouncing around in my head. The next morning I set out to solve the mystery of Pandora's Box. I tracked down the address of the company listed on Amaya's clandestine bank account and phoned to book an appointment with the owner and was pleasantly surprised to be granted one. *Things are looking up*, I thought. *Things will go my way. Soon the mystery would be solved, and we can go back to how it was, before.*

Showered and dressed, I caught a taxi to the building in Sumida, which was very elegant, streamlined and monochromatic. Usually, I prefer bright colours and *kawaii* over minimalism, but I liked the architecture. It made me feel calm.

"Ohayō Misutā Tanaka," said a handsome man in chinos. They weren't the cheap kind. "I'm Yamamura—Yama for short. Thanks for coming in today."

He led me from reception to a white, high-ceilinged room with large windows where the air was fragrant with the jasmine tea that was steaming on the table. I could see the Tokyo Skytree in the distance. We sat, and Yamamura steepled his manicured fingers and looked at me in a friendly way. "What can I do for you today?"

I hesitated. How does one tell a charming stranger that he had invaded his wife's privacy to find this place?

"Go ahead," he said. "I'm listening. I'm sure I can help you."

My toes were wriggling inside my shoes. "I would very much like to know what this company does. There is no information on the internet."

"Ah," Yama said. "Of course. Have you recently lost a loved one?"

Again, I hesitated. In a way, I had. I'd lost the idea of Amaya as the perfect wife, and our relationship as honest and resilient. Still, I knew this was not what the man was asking.

"No," I replied, wondering where this exciting conversation was going.

Yamamura sprang up. He had lots of energy in his body; I could tell he loved his job.

"This is the Family Romance of Neurotics," he said. "We specialise in companionship."

My jaw suddenly began to ache. My heart surged, but not in a good way. "You're an escort agency?"

Yamamura coughed in alarm. "Oh, no," he assured me. "Not at all. Not one bit. We are a kind, wholesome enterprise that helps people."

This made me feel marginally better. "People who need ... company?" I asked.

"We enlist stand-ins," Yama said. "Terrific actors who can pretend to be your mother, your daughter, your best friend. We have actors who enjoy the cinema who will go with you to a film if you don't enjoy going alone. Same goes for dinners, travelling, or just quiet time at home. We have people who you can hire to cry at funerals—or weddings!—or if your boss needs to shout at someone, we offer that service, too. We're open and flexible. The possibilities are endless."

. . .

On the way home, my mind was racing, imagining Amaya in these situations. I could picture her standing in a cemetery, holding a black umbrella and mourning like in one of those melancholic American films, tears falling with the soft rain. I imagined her laughing at someone's bad jokes over a sashimi platter, or cooking one of her excellent dishes—shirataki with mushrooms, or yakisoba.

She was a wonderful person. I'm sure she was very good at making people feel better about life. Amaya had a way of lighting up a room. Perhaps a room wasn't enough for her; maybe she thought it was her duty to light up other peoples' lives. Perhaps it was my duty to allow her to do that. I decided that I would tell her everything and let her know that I supported her generosity of spirit. Secrets in a marriage are corrosive, aren't they? Yes, I had felt a stab of acrimony when I discovered her secret phone and bank account, but I understand why she hid it from me. I needed to apologise to her for sneaking into her phone.

When I arrived home, I got out my rainbow duster and finished cleaning the office. It felt good. Then I remembered the Hello Kitty flash drive and went to get it from our bedroom, but it was gone.

What had been on the disk? Photos, lists, personal information. Perhaps the kind of data that The Family Romance of Neurotics would supply one of their employees. One of the hobbies listed was my love of beekeeping. I had been to every bee talk and workshop in the city but had never seen Amaya before that day we met. The necklace she wore had looked brand new. I realised that her sitting down next to me at the workshop had not been an accident. My parents' nagging echoed in my head. First, it was "You need to find someone!" and then it turned into "We want grandchildren!" They'd chime it over and over. The knowledge of what they had done crashed in on me like a tsunami, and I just sat there for a long time, trying to process the information. I wished I had never found that disk; wished it had stayed buried in its black box at the top of the cupboard. I couldn't change the past, but I could pretend that I had never found it. I washed my hands, straightened my shirt, and strode down to the kitchen where delicious aromas swirled in the air. Amaya had already begun cooking.

"Amaya-chan!" I said, and we hugged like a regular happily married couple. I decided I could make it work. I offered to chop the onions, and she passed me the board. She was a good actress, I thought. Very talented. But I could be a good actor, too.

DEAR READER

Thank you for staying with me on this journey!

I love hearing from readers, so please don't hesitate to get in touch. I'm only an email away!

If you'd care to review this collection, I'd especially like to know which story was your favourite, and if there are any in particular you'd like to see turned into novels.

Thank you for supporting my work!

Janita

janita@pulpbooks.co.za

www.jt-lawrence.com

~

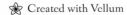